A Bright Idea?

"I can't believe all the stuff the mermaid did yesterday," I say to Stacey when we meet at the broken water fountain before school on Tuesday morning.

Stacey pulls the mermaid out of her backpack. "Time to trade her back," she says. "I plugged her in extra early last night so she could do even bigger stuff today."

I tuck the mermaid into my backpack.

Stacey gets that far-off look like she did yesterday when she asked the mermaid to make our math quiz go away. She puts her hand on my backpack and says, "Dear Mermaid, make something extra *good* happen for Ida and me today!"

Stacey takes her hand away and smiles. "Now we just have to be on the lookout for something extra good to happen. Just for the two of us!"

I pick up my backpack and slip it on. "Are you sure an *evil* mermaid can make *good* things happen?" I ask.

Stacey nods. "She's only part evil," she says. "Like most things."

Other books by Julie Bowe

My Last Best Friend
My Best Frenemy

My New Best Friend

Julie Bowe

sandpiper

Houghton Mifflin Harcourt

Boston New York

My thanks to . . .

My editor, Kathy Dawson, who always stands at the ready with a big supply of encouragement, enthusiasm, and sticky notes.

My agent, Steven Chudney, for his guidance and friendship.

Everyone at Harcourt including Barbara Fisch, Sarah Shealy, and Kia Neri for their marketing help. And book designer April Ward, who gets all the credit when kids tell me, "I love the way you typed your books."

Illustrator Jana Christy, for giving Ida a face that so perfectly matches her heart.

Friends and family for cheering me on.

And my special thanks to Makena, Leslie, Julia, Dany, Jessica, Taylor, Maggie, Carly, Grainne, Claire, Brianna, Skylar, Alaina, Lauren, Ashley, Kellie, Megan, Kate, Justine, Katie, Bonnie, Kaitlyn, and Kimberly, who sent me my first fan mail and asked, "What are you working on next?" This is it, girls. I hope you like it!

Illustrations © 2008 by Jana Christy
The text of this book is set in Esprit Book.

The Library of Congress has cataloged the hardcover edition as follows:
Bowe, Julie, 1962–
My new best friend/Julie Bowe.
p. cm.
Summary: Fourth grader Ida May and her new best friend, Stacey Merriweather, discover a mermaid night-light that they believe can grant wishes.
[1. Best friends—Fiction. 2. Friendship—Fiction. 3. Schools—Fiction.] I. Title.
PZ7.B671943Myg   2008
[Fic]—dc22   2007046005

ISBN 978-0-15-206498-3
ISBN 978-0-547-32869-0 pb

Manufactured in the United States of America
EB 10
4500712282

For my family—Aaron, Micah, & Eli

Rusty

Mr. Crow

Tom

Dominic

Quinn

Meeka

me!

Stacey

My New Best Friend

Chapter
1

I'm Ida May and I have a lot to be thankful for.

- I have not dropped my lunch tray once since the start of fourth grade.
- I have only tripped twice in public.
- Dodgeball season is almost over.
- So is our science unit on dissecting worms.

I'm thankful for my teacher, Mr. Crow, even though he makes us slice open worms and pin back their skin. Because he doesn't make us touch their insides if we don't want to. And he always comes up with new ways to keep us from getting too bored with school. For example, he makes us learn how to spell big words like *influenza,* which is what you get if you breathe in too many bad germs, and *catastrophe,* which is what you get if things don't go the way you planned.

Also, he reads to us every day. Not baby books, either. Lately, he's been reading us Greek stories about gods and goddesses and the creatures that work for them. Actually, they're Greek *myths*. *Myth* is a Greek word for *made-up story*. Like the one about the god Apollo driving a chariot across the sky when really it's just the sun. And other myths about pretty nymphs and singing muses who aren't as powerful as goddesses but, still, they can get you to do things that you don't exactly want to do. Mr. Crow says a myth is true if you believe it's true.

When Mr. Crow is done reading myths to us we will get to have a Greek Day. We'll even get to act out our favorite myths and invite our families to come and watch. Personally, I'd rather draw a picture of a myth than act it out, but sometimes in fourth grade you don't get to choose.

I'm thankful for the usual stuff, too. Like my mom and my dad and my sock monkey, George.

But most of all, I'm thankful that my new best friend, Stacey Merriweather, has moved to my town: Purdee, Wisconsin. Permanently. She's spending the day at my house because we're getting ready to go to Brooke Morgan's costume birthday party later this afternoon. Brooke invited our whole class. Even the boys.

Even Jenna Drews.

I'm *not* so thankful that Brooke invited Jenna to the party. That's because Jenna is the kind of person who would pin back your skin if she could. Then she would take something sharp and poke at all the stuff you'd rather keep hidden. Stuff like spilling your lunch tray. And tripping on the bus.

I glance across my bedroom at Stacey. She's digging through a big box of old costumes my mom hauled down from the attic. We're trying to decide what to be for Brooke's costume birthday party.

"How about princesses?" Stacey asks. She pulls two sparkly dresses out of the box.

I glance at the dresses, fall back across my bed, and pop a Choco-chunk into my mouth. "Too third grade," I say.

Stacey nods and digs some more. "Pirates recently marooned on a desert island?" She holds up a red bandana and a black eye patch.

I shake my head. "Randi and Rusty are being pirates. They'll say we copied. And you can cross beauty queens off your list," I add. "That's what Brooke, Meeka, and Jolene are going to be."

Stacey nods again. "What about Jenna?" she asks.

"What about her?" I reply, even though Jenna Drews is not my favorite topic of discussion.

Stacey folds the red bandana into a triangle and fits it across her nose and mouth, tying it in back. "The last time I asked Jenna what she was going to be for Brooke's party she said we should be something together, and I said I couldn't because I was going to be something with you, and then she just stomped off." Stacey holds up her fingers like pistols. "Bandits?" she says from behind her mask.

I shake my head. "Joey, Quinn, and Zane are going to be the Three Musketeers. If they see us dressed like bandits we'll get chased all over Purdee." I toss a Choco-chunk into the air and try to catch it with my teeth even though my dad, the orthodontist, discourages teeth catching. "As for Jenna," I say, after the Choco-chunk bounces off my nose, "she's so crazy about healthy stuff she'll probably wrap herself in paper and go as a granola bar."

Stacey giggles and pulls off her mask. "We could be ballet dancers," she says, lifting her arms and doing a graceful spin.

I sigh. Before Stacey's parents got divorced, she took ballet lessons. After she and her mom moved to Purdee, Stacey's grandmother signed her up for lessons here. Now Stacey dances off to Miss Woo's Dance Studio with Jenna, Brooke, Meeka, and Jolene once a week. "But I can't dance," I say.

"I could teach you," Stacey offers, making her big brown eyes go all wide and hopeful.

I just shake my head. "I've never done a pirouette on purpose in my life. I don't want to start now."

Stacey slumps. "Well, then," she says, pulling a ragged felt hat and a pair of beat-up boots from the box. "How about orphans?" Stacey puts the hat on her head and gets a far-off look in her eyes. It's the kind of look she always gets when her brain is churning up a new story. "Orphans...," she says, "who run away from a rat-infested

5

orphanage, which is run by an evil, orphan-hating woman."

"How come she runs an orphanage if she hates orphans?" I ask. "I mean, couldn't she run a bakery or a hardware store or some other orphanless thing instead?"

Stacey shakes her head. "It doesn't work that way," she says. "There's got to be someone who hates you or you don't have a story." Stacey adjusts her felt hat and continues. "We hide at the home of a friendly hermit and his pet...um... monkey." She pauses to pick up my sock monkey, George, who is lying on the floor next to my bed.

"Does the hermit like orphans?" I ask.

"Yes," Stacey says.

"And the monkey?"

Stacey nods. "The monkey likes orphans, too."

I smile at George even though he doesn't look too happy to be playing a part in this story.

"Only we discover that the hermit is really a *wizard*," Stacey says to George, like he's listening. "Plus, the hermit's pet monkey is really our rich *uncle*, who got put under a spell by...the *evil orphanage woman* who is really a *witch*!"

Stacey does an excited little gasp and starts

6

twirling George by his long, skinny arms. "So the hermit/wizard breaks the evil spell and changes the monkey back into our uncle and we are very rich and happy forever. The End."

Stacey leans back against my bed, looking like she just ran around the block.

I toss Stacey a Choco-chunk. "That story was even better than the one you told about Mr. Crow getting shipwrecked when he was two and being raised by dolphins," I say.

Stacey smiles at me. "Thanks," she says back, popping the candy into her mouth. "So it's decided? We'll be runaway orphans for Brooke's party?"

I think about what that would be like, showing up at Brooke's party in ragged clothes and smudgy cheeks. It reminds me of another time Stacey made me get dressed up with her in sparkly dresses, red lipstick, and blue eye shadow. Then we went to see a movie about an ordinary girl who found out she was really a princess. While I waited in the lobby for Stacey to go to the bathroom, people kept looking at me funny. Then Meeka and Jolene showed up. When they first saw me they giggled and made a big deal about my costume, just like they were supposed to. But then Meeka suddenly gasped and said all embarrassed, "Oh my gosh, Ida. Did you dress like that on purpose?"

I said, "No, of course not! It's just a costume," over and over again but the more I said it, the more it sounded like I was making it up. They left the theater before Stacey got back so I never got to prove that we were both dressing up just to be silly.

I roll over on my stomach and think about dressing up in old, ragged clothes. I think about people looking at me funny, even though it *is* a costume party. And me feeling like I have to say, "I'm a runaway orphan" the whole time just to be sure they get that I'm dressing up. As I do, I study the box that the costumes are in. CHUMMY BATHROOM TISSUE is printed on it. Apparently, my parents buy toilet paper in bulk.

The box gives me an idea.

I look at Stacey. "Orphans are okay, but maybe we should be something that no one else will think to be. Something they will know right away is a costume."

"Like what?" Stacey asks.

I study the box again. "Let's be ... outhouses."

"*Outhouses?*"

"Yeah," I say, sitting up on my knees. "We can paint boxes to look like old-fashioned outhouses." I pause to grab my sketchbook and a pencil from my nightstand. I start drawing the picture that's inside my head. "And add cardboard roofs," I continue. "And cut half-moon holes out of the front to see through. And paint HIS and HERS on the fake doors." I glance up at Stacey. "You can even be the HERS if you want."

I hold up my sketchbook so Stacey can see the drawing. She takes time to look it over. Then she gives me my favorite smile and says, "Okay!"

We race up the narrow steps that lead to my attic. I flick on the light switch, and a dusty bulb that dangles from the ceiling starts to glow. We search around the dim room for boxes, being careful not to bash our heads on the low rafters.

We find two boxes with real outhouse potential. One of them is filled with old baby toys and scribbled up books and carnival leftovers. We start emptying the stuff onto a shelf.

"That's everything," Stacey says, pulling a

teddy bear leg, a headless Barbie, and a lucky horseshoe from the box. She tosses them onto the shelf with everything else. "Except for *this*."

I look inside the box and see a mermaid night-light. The mermaid is perched on a pink plastic rock, surrounded by blue plastic waves. An electrical cord pokes out of her green plastic tail. She smiles at us pleasantly.

"That's strange," I say. "I don't remember ever having a mermaid night-light."

Stacey pulls the mermaid out of the box. "Let's see if it still works," she says.

We carry the mermaid to a workbench my dad has set up at one end of the attic. It's covered with tools I've never actually seen him use. I clear away a little space and Stacey sets the mermaid down. Then I pick up the cord and plug it into an outlet.

"She works!" Stacey cries as the mermaid begins to glow.

I turn the mermaid around so we can see her face. As soon as I do we both gasp and jump back, banging our heads on a rafter.

The mermaid's pleasant smile has turned into a glowing grin. It's the kind of grin you see on a clown's face in a scary movie right after he steps out from behind a greasy black tree and revs up a chain saw.

We stand there too afraid to move, staring at the glowing mermaid.

"S-s-stacey?" I whisper.

"Y-y-yes?" she whispers back.

"Her *lips* moved."

We scream like spider monkeys and run right out of the attic and down the narrow steps and hide under my bed for about three hours.

Then we dare each other to go back and unplug her. This goes on for about another three hours.

Then we *both* go back, clinging to each other and scream-laughing the whole way.

We rip the cord out of the socket. The mermaid smiles pleasantly again. But we know as soon as we plug her in she will turn back into the Evil One.

"We should make a club," I say.

"What kind of club?" Stacey asks.

"The Secret Mermaid Club," I reply.

"Oooo . . . that's a good idea," Stacey says. "We need a club pledge. Something like . . ." Stacey places her hand on the mermaid's head. "I solemnly swear to light this mermaid every night no matter how much the sight of her evil, glowing grin makes me want to pee my pants."

"Perfect," I say. "We'll take turns keeping her." Then I put my hand on top of Stacey's and say the pledge, too.

"Plus, we'll keep the club a secret," I say.

"From everyone," Stacey adds.

We take our hands off the mermaid, but I can still feel my fingers tingling.

Chapter

2

"We found her in your attic," Stacey says, picking up the mermaid. "You take her first."

"Okay," I say, taking the mermaid from her. "But just for one night. Then it's your turn."

We carry the mermaid to my room very carefully, like she's carved from finger Jell-O. We set her on my windowsill.

"Now what?" I ask.

"Now we light her every night," Stacey says.

"And then what?"

"Then we have our club meetings and talk about what difference it makes," Stacey explains.

"Difference?"

"Like if stuff starts happening now that we've brought her back to life. Like in the movies."

"What movies?" I ask.

"The movies me and my brother used to watch

before he moved in with our dad. When we were a family. The ones with evil spells, and runaway orphans, and stuff."

I nod like I know exactly what she's talking about. But really, I don't have much experience with runaway orphans and evil spells and not being a family.

We collapse on my bedroom floor and eat half a bag of Choco-chunks.

Then we go back to the attic and get the two boxes.

"This attic would make a great secret clubhouse," I say, looking around at all the stuff my parents store up here. "We could use that old crib mattress for a couch and that piano bench for a table." I walk over to the bench my mom's piano students sat on until it got too wobbly. I lift the lid on the bench. "We can even hide stuff in here!"

Stacey looks around. "Doesn't your dad come up here to use his tools and stuff?"

"Not since last spring when he hammered his thumb so bad he had to go to the emergency room. Now my mom does all the hammering in the family. She keeps her hammer in a junk drawer in the kitchen."

Stacey nods and looks around the attic again. "Our secret clubhouse," she says, taking it all in.

I nod and close the lid on the bench. "Just for us."

We haul the boxes downstairs and get the first outhouse mostly done before we realize it's too small for either of us to wear without suffocating. So we start over with two bigger boxes. We get my mom to help us glue on the cardboard roofs and cut out the arm holes and half moons. Then my dad helps us paint the boxes to look like wood, but they don't require any hammering. We write HIS and HERS on the front of them.

Then we lie across my bed, toss Choco-chunks to George, and make up evil mermaid stories while the boxes dry.

We try them on.

They are the best costumes ever.

"Say 'cheese'!" Mom tells us later that day from behind her camera.

"Cheese!" me and Stacey say, smiling through the half moons in our outhouses.

Mom clicks a picture. Then she hands us two matching gift bags. We each got Brooke one sock, one glove, and one earring, just to be funny. "Let's go party!" Mom says.

"Can we stop by the Purdee Good on the way to Brooke's?" Stacey asks. "Kelli's working and she wants to see our costumes."

Stacey calls her mom Kelli just like the rest of us. The Purdee Good is a café where she's a waitress. It's named after our town, Purdee. Plus, they serve purdee good food there. Get it?

"Sure," Mom says. "Oh, and there's one more thing...," she adds.

"What?" I ask.

The doorbell rings.

Mom walks over to the door and peeks out the window. Then she looks back at us. "*This*," she says and opens the door.

There stands Jenna Drews and her little sister, Rachel.

"Hi, girls!" Mom says, like she was expecting them.

"Hi, Mrs. May," Rachel says back. "Thank you for inviting us." Rachel's wearing a white ballet leotard with white netting wrapped around it. A flowery wreath is on her head. She reminds me of a statue I saw in a park once. Only Rachel doesn't have any bird poop on her.

Jenna is wearing a green leotard with fake vines stuck to it. Bugs and butterflies are painted on her face. Her hair, which is usually braided, is loose and crimped. It hangs over her shoulders like lasagna noodles. It's dyed the color of cooked peas.

Mom turns to me and Stacey. "I didn't have a chance to tell you," she says.

"Tell us what?" I ask.

"Mr. and Mrs. Drews had something come up at the last minute, so Jenna and Rachel are going to the party with us!"

My chin practically drops out of my half moon.

"Great!" Stacey says, all cheerful.

"Stacey?" Jenna says. "Is that *you*?"

"Yep," Stacey says back. "I'm an outhouse! It was Ida's idea." She gives me a smile.

Jenna gives me a look. "Figures," she says.

"Um...what are you supposed to be?" I ask Jenna. "A talking log?"

Jenna glares at me. "For your information," she says, "I'm *Gaia*."

"*Who-a?*"

Jenna rolls her eyes. "*Gai-*a," she replies. "Goddess of the Earth. *Hello?* Mr. Crow just read a myth about her last week."

"Oh," I say. "Sorry. Wrong number."

Rachel tugs on Jenna's vine. "*I* want to be an outhouse," she says.

"No, Rachel," Jenna says back. "You're a *muse.*"

"But I don't want to be a moose," Rachel says. "Not unless I get to wear antlers."

Jenna rolls her eyes again. "Not a *moose,* Rachel. A *muse.* You sing and dance and do whatever I tell you."

"I want to be an outhouse," Rachel grumbles.

"I'm not taking a stinky old outhouse to Brooke's party," Jenna says. "You're lucky I'm taking you at all," she adds. "It's not like you were invited."

Rachel swallows hard. Her bottom lip starts to tremble.

I turn to my mom. "We *do* have an extra box," I say.

My mom smiles at me and nods.

"What *extra box?*" Jenna says.

"This one," Mom says and disappears into the kitchen. A moment later she returns with the too-small outhouse. She fits it over Rachel's head.

"It's perfect," Stacey says, smiling at Rachel.

"Wait," I say and bump my way to the kitchen. I grab a black marker out of the junk drawer. I bump my way back and write MINE under Rachel's half-moon chin.

Rachel steps back and smiles at all of us. "How do I look?" she asks.

"Very a-*muse*-ing," I say.

Stacey giggles.

Jenna snorts and shakes back her green hair. "Can we *go* now? My makeup is starting to melt."

"I'll grab my keys and meet you at the van," Mom says.

We head out the door. Jenna barges to the front of the pack, practically knocking Rachel right out of her box.

I grab Rachel's arm to steady her. "Are you okay?" I ask.

"Yep," she says. "I'm not breakable."

"It's a good thing I showed up," Jenna says when we get to the van.

"Um...how do you figure?" I ask.

"Just look at you two," she says, giving me and Stacey the once-over. "Going to a party dressed like that. How are you going to drink punch? Your arms barely poke out. Plus, you'll be bumping into people and tripping over furniture the whole time."

"We'll manage," I say as we pile our boxes into the back of the van.

Jenna lifts her buggy chin. "You need me," she says, hopping into the front seat.

"Um...no, we don't," I mumble and hop in back.

We stop at the Purdee Good on our way to the party. Kelli takes pictures of us to send to Stacey's dad.

"Can't your dad even show up to take his own pictures?" Jenna asks Stacey as we head back to the van.

"It's not like that," Stacey says. "He wants to be here...it's just...it's complicated."

Jenna huffs. "I'd never let my parents split up."

"It's not like I had a *choice*, Jenna," Stacey replies.

"Still," Jenna says, "it's not going to happen in *my* family."

It's a good thing Brooke has a big house because lots of people are at her party. Almost all the kids from our class are there, plus a bunch of strangers who look a lot like Brooke with their dark, shiny hair and perfectly straight teeth. Relatives.

Jenna pulls Stacey through the crowd like a box kite on a string. She feeds her punch and treats. She even yanks down streamers and balloons and decorates Stacey until she looks more like a parade float than an outhouse.

Every time I try to get within bumping distance of Stacey, Jenna drags her away to another part of the house. Rachel goes off to play with one of Brooke's little cousins. I just grab a handful of chips from the snack table, lean against a wall, and pull my arms inside my box. I eat chips and watch the party through my half moon. It isn't long before one of Brooke's relatives stops right in front of me, blocking my view. She gulps down the last of her punch, sets the empty cup on top of me, and walks away.

"Use a coaster next time," I mumble.

When it's time for Brooke to open her presents, Jenna puts herself in charge of handing them to her. She gives Brooke the gift she brought first. "It's a diary," Jenna says before Brooke even gets all the wrapping paper ripped off. "My dad helped me make it. We put water and old newspapers into a blender and churned it into *pulp*. Then we spread the pulp on a screen and let it dry to make the pages." Jenna takes the diary from Brooke and opens it up to show everyone. Each page looks like a pan of oatmeal.

"Um...thanks," Brooke says.

"You're welcome," Jenna replies. She props the diary up on a shelf like it should be in a museum.

Next, Jenna hands Brooke Stacey's gift, but not mine.

"Um...," I say, tapping on the inside of my box. "That's actually a two-part gift."

No one hears me. All I can do is watch as Brooke pulls one sock, glove, and earring out of the gift bag from Stacey. She does a puzzled look. But Stacey is too busy giggling with Meeka and Jolene to tell Brooke that the rest of her present is in the bag from her *best friend*. Me. Ida May.

When my mom finally shows up to take us home, Mrs. Drews shows up, too. I guess her meeting with Mr. Drews got done early. She insists on giving Stacey a ride home to make up for any trouble Jenna and Rachel caused my mom.

"They were no trouble at all, Pauline," Mom tells her.

"That's right," I chime in, not wanting her to take Stacey.

"I insist," Mrs. Drews says, herding Stacey, Jenna, and Rachel down the sidewalk.

Jenna shoots a satisfied look at me as Stacey ditches her outhouse and climbs into Jenna's car.

Jenna climbs in next to Stacey and closes the door.

I pull off my box and wave good-bye to Stacey as they drive away.

Stacey doesn't see me because Jenna's big, green head is in the way.

As soon as I get home I stomp upstairs. I change into my grumpy-face pajamas. I rip open my birthday treat bag and yank out two fun-size candy bars. I crush them with my bare hands before

I eat them. I stomp to the bathroom and practically brush the bristles right off my MAY ORTHODONTICS toothbrush.

Then I stomp back to my room. George gives me a concerned sort of look.

"Because Jenna Drews is a jerk," I say. "And that's the *truth*."

George remains calm.

I turn away and catch a glimpse of the mermaid night-light. She smiles pleasantly at me.

I study her for a minute. Then I walk over and pick her up. "Just one evil spell," I say.

I set her on the windowsill again and turn her face toward Jenna Drews's house. "Chicken pox...hairy spots...ugly warts that itch a lot..."

I pick up her cord and plug it in.

Then I dive for my bed and hide under my covers before her evil, glowing grin makes me pee my pants.

Chapter

3

The next morning I get dressed, make my bed, set George on my pillow, and walk over to the mermaid. Even in the morning she looks spooky. I wonder if she zapped Jenna with any evil spells while I was sleeping.

"Let's find out," I say, unplugging her. Before I put her inside my backpack, I wrap a red bandana around her. Then I head downstairs.

When I get to the bus stop, Quinn and his little sister, Tess, are already there. Tess waves to Rachel, who is walking down the sidewalk with Jenna. Rachel waves back because she and Tess are best kindergarten friends.

I study Jenna as she gets closer, looking for signs of chicken pox or warts. But all I see are her two bobbing braids. They are still bright green.

"How come you got green hair?" Tess asks Jenna when she gets to the bus stop.

Jenna's jaw tightens and her cheeks heat up. "Because the dye wouldn't wash out."

"She washed it *fifteen* times," Rachel says, giggling.

Quinn snorts.

Jenna scowls.

I think I feel something shift inside my backpack.

"Um...anything else?" I ask, looking Jenna over. "Itchy spots? Suspicious bumps?"

Jenna turns her scowl on me. "Of course not," she says. "I used all-natural *henna* hair dye, not battery acid."

"*Henna Jenna,*" I mumble. Quinn hears me and snorts again.

"Only she didn't read the directions first," Rachel says.

This time Jenna gives her sister a shove.

The bus arrives and we climb on. Kids turn and point at Jenna.

"Look! The creature from the *Green Lagoon*!"

Fake screams.

Fake faints.

Jenna pushes through and drops into the very back seat. She scrunches down so all you can see is the top of her green head.

I scoot into another seat, unzip my backpack, and peek at the mermaid.

She smiles back at me.

When I get to school I grab Stacey's arm and pull her to the broken water fountain.

"Guess what?" I say as soon as we get there.

"What?" she says back.

"Last night, when I got home, I wished an evil spell on Jenna, and now her hair is *green*. Probably forever!" I unzip my backpack and show her the mermaid.

Stacey studies the mermaid for a moment. "I knew lighting her would make a difference," she says.

I nod. "So it's for real, right? Me wishing an evil spell and Jenna ending up with permanently green hair? I mean, it *can't* be. But just look at Jenna!"

"The only way to know for sure is to do another spell," Stacey says.

My heart jiggles inside my chest. "On who? Jenna? Because I was thinking red spots would go good with her green hair. Sort of an early Christmas present."

Stacey narrows her eyes, thinking. "I know," she says all mysterious. "Quick! Follow me."

I follow Stacey down the hall and into the girls' bathroom. She heads to the last stall, pulls me in, and locks the latch. "Take her out," she whispers.

I pull the mermaid from my backpack. "Don't we need to plug her in?" I ask.

"Did you plug her in last night?" Stacey asks.

I nod.

"Then she's good to go," Stacey says. "As long as we plug her in every night, she'll help us during the day."

I nod again. "How do you know so much about this stuff?" I ask, handing over the mermaid. "I mean, sometimes it seems like you've been nine a lot longer than me."

Stacey shrugs. "I just do," she says. "I even know stuff my mom doesn't know."

"Like what?"

"Like my dad has a new girlfriend. Tanya. She's always around when I stay with him. But my brother isn't. I guess Jake doesn't like her as much as my dad does."

"Do you like her?" I ask.

Stacey shrugs. "She's okay. But you can't tell Kelli. It would make her sad if she knew about Tanya."

"Okay," I say. "I won't tell."

Stacey gives me a nod. Then she looks at the mermaid again.

"So, what are we going to make her do?" I ask.

Stacey gets that far-off look in her eyes. Then she gives me a sly smile. "What's the worst thing about school?" she asks.

"Um ... dodgeball? Salisbury steak? Times tables?"

"Bingo," Stacey says. She puts her hand on the mermaid's head and closes her eyes. "Dear Mermaid," she says. "Make today's math quiz go away. Make Mr. Crow spill tea all over it. Make him use it to line the hamster cage. Make him accidentally run it through the *paper shredder.*"

Stacey opens her eyes and blinks at me.

I blink back. Then I put my hand on top of hers. "Only don't let him shred his hand or anything."

The bell rings as soon as we get to our coat-room. Everyone hurries to hang up their stuff. I walk to my desk, sit down, and glance at Stacey. She's sitting across from me in the next row. Jenna sits right behind her in perfect shoulder-tapping, note-passing distance. I feel my stomach squirm.

When we first started fourth grade, we sat in clusters. But Mr. Crow likes to change things around so now instead of staring at Rusty's, Tom's, and Randi's faces, I get to stare at the back of Zane Howard's shaved head. This may sound like a bad view, but actually it's coming in handy. That's because Zane had an accident with a bunk bed when he was little. His top-bunk double flip got him seventeen stitches in the back of his head and a scar that's shaped like New Jersey. New Jersey is one of the states I can never name on the map, so as long as Zane Howard sits in front of me I'm going to do a lot better in social studies.

Mr. Crow is at the board. He writes MATH QUIZ TODAY in big, bold letters. I glance at the coatroom. I swear I see my backpack jiggle.

As soon as everyone takes their seat Mr. Crow sits down at his computer to do attendance. It takes him a while to get started because he's busy rubbing his forehead like he has a headache.

"Is Dylan Adams here?" he asks.

"Right here!" Dylan says back.

Mr. Crow nods and rubs his head again. "How about Dylan Anderson?"

"Here!" the other Dylan replies.

Mr. Crow clicks his mouse and then wipes his hand across his forehead. He takes a sip of tea and makes a face like he swallowed sawdust. "Joey Carpenter?"

"Here!" Joey replies.

Mr. Crow nods and clicks again. He pulls a handkerchief out of his pocket and leans his face into it.

"Is Jenna here?" he mumbles through the handkerchief.

"Yes, Mr. Crow, I'm right here," Jenna says.

I feel a tap on my shoulder. I turn around and

see Quinn's goofy grin. "Henna Jenna's hard to miss!" he whispers loudly.

Randi gives us a glance. "*Henna* Jenna?" she asks.

I poke a thumb toward Jenna. "She used something called *henna* to dye her hair. Now it won't wash out."

Randi grins at Jenna. "Hey, Henna Jenna," she whispers loudly. "Did you dye your hair or is that a turtle sleeping on your head?"

Randi cracks up.

So does Quinn.

Jenna does not. She gives us a sneer. I pull my chin inside my collar and grin.

"Zane How...*How*..." Mr. Crow pushes away from his computer. "Excuse...me, everyone. I'm not...feeling...very well." His voice sounds spongy. And his face looks like my Grandma May's green-bean casserole. He clutches his stomach and stumbles out the door.

"What's wrong with Mr. Crow?" Meeka asks.

"Looks like a bad case of indigestion," Tom says.

"Barf-O-Rama!" Rusty shouts.

"*Eeeeewwww!*" the whole class chimes in.

Some of the boys start staggering around, making barf sounds.

Some of the girls stagger around, making barf sounds back.

Brooke groans. She looks like she could be the next Barf-O-Rama contestant.

Jenna marches to the front of the classroom. "Take your seats!" she shouts. "Just because Mr. Crow left doesn't mean you can start acting crazy!"

Everyone keeps fake-barfing on each other's shoes.

"Make them...stop..." Brooke moans. She clutches her desk like it's the safety bar on a Tilt-a-Whirl.

Jenna's eyes dart around at all the barfers. "I am a junior Girl Scout!" she shouts. "Do what I say!"

"What're you gonna do if we don't?" Randi asks. "Toss your *cookies*?"

Randi laughs and fake-barfs on Dominic's desk.

Jenna shoots a scowl at Randi. She grabs Mr.

Crow's ruler and starts waving it around. "Zane, get down from the bookcase! Rusty, take your finger out of your throat! Meeka, stop moaning!"

But no one listens to her. That's because it's hard to take orders from a person with green hair. Even if she is a junior Girl Scout.

Jenna is in the middle of listing her qualifications to be in charge (*"I earned my Safety Sense Brownie badge last year and I'm just three good deeds away from my junior Girl Scout Model Citizen pin, and..."*) when a large dark shadow creeps through the doorway. It's followed by the large dark body of our music teacher, Mrs. Madson.

Mrs. Madson steps into the classroom. She crosses her meaty arms over her black dress. She scans the scene from behind her bat-wing glasses while tapping the toe of one blood-red shoe. When she spots Zane on top of the bookcase her black eyebrows arch up until they almost touch her equally black hair.

"Zane Howard!" she shouts. "Get. Down. *Now!*"

Zane freezes. His eyes lock with Mrs. Madson's and he melts to the floor.

"Everyone, back to your desks!" she barks. Half a second later, everyone is back in their desks.

This concludes today's Barf-O-Rama, I say to myself.

Jenna sets down Mr. Crow's ruler and marches over to Mrs. Madson. "They're all yours," she says, shaking back her green braids.

Mrs. Madson studies Jenna over the top of her glasses. "Thank you," she says.

Jenna gives her a quick nod and marches back to her desk.

Mrs. Madson steps to the front of the classroom. "Ladies and gentlemen," she says. "I regret to inform you that your teacher has gone home unexpectedly. I have been asked to step in until Mrs. Eddy, your substitute, arrives." Mrs. Madson scans the room slowly. "Are there any questions?"

Tom raises his hand. "What about our math quiz?"

Everyone shoots a look at Tom.

"Math quiz?" Mrs. Madson replies.

"We were supposed to have one this morning," Tom blabs some more.

Mrs. Madson smoothes her large hands over

her black dress, thinking over this information. "Due to the unexpected circumstances," she says, "your math quiz has been *canceled* for today."

I do a gasp and glance at Stacey.

She gasps and glances back.

"*The mermaid,*" we whisper at the exact same time.

Chapter

4

You might think casting a spell that makes your teacher come down with a sudden case of the up-chucks would be all an evil mermaid could dish out for one day. The truth is, evil mermaid night-lights are a lot more powerful than they let on. I know because all day yesterday the mermaid kept making bad things happen.

Me and Stacey didn't even have to wish for a spell on Rusty Smith, but the mermaid still made him get caught sticking a KICK ME sign to our principal's back.

Then Joey Carpenter tied one of Jolene's shoelaces to her desk and when her big brother found out Joey got stuck inside a sixth-grade locker for almost all of art.

And best of all, Jenna Drews got kicked out of the cafeteria for throwing her tomato-tofu sandwich at Quinn. She said she did it because Quinn poked her ear with a fork. But Quinn claimed he thought Jenna's green head was the Salad of the Day and shouldn't be held responsible for his actions.

Actually, I might have been responsible for the tofu-throwing spell a tiny bit because right before it happened I mentioned to Stacey that I wouldn't mind if the mermaid did something to make Jenna lose a few Girl Scout badges.

"I can't believe all the stuff the mermaid did yesterday," I say to Stacey when we meet at the broken water fountain before school on Tuesday morning.

Stacey pulls the mermaid out of her backpack. "Time to trade her back," she says. "I plugged her in extra early last night so she could do even bigger stuff today."

"What could be bigger than Rusty getting afternoon detention? Or Jenna having to eat her lunch in the office?" I tuck the mermaid into my backpack.

Stacey thinks for a moment. Then she gets that far-off look like she did yesterday when she asked the mermaid to make our math quiz go away. She puts her hand on my backpack and says, "Dear Mermaid, make something extra *good* happen for Ida and me today!"

Stacey takes her hand away and smiles. "Now we just have to be on the lookout for something extra good to happen. Just for the two of us!"

I pick up my backpack and slip it on. "Are you sure an *evil* mermaid can make *good* things happen?" I ask.

Stacey nods. "She's only part evil," she says. "Like most things."

The bell rings and we head to our classroom. I smile the whole way, even though there's a mermaid poking me in the back.

When we get to the classroom our sub from yesterday, Mrs. Eddy, is sitting at Mr. Crow's desk.

"Hi, Mrs. Eddy," I say. "Is Mr. Crow still sick?"

"Yes, he is," Mrs. Eddy replies. "He must have caught that flu bug that's been going around."

"Or that *spell*," I mumble to myself and head to my desk.

39

All morning, I'm on the lookout for something extra good to happen. Unless you count Tom Sanders not mentioning our canceled math quiz again, only regular things happen. Reading. Social studies. Math. Jenna making us play dodgeball at recess. Salisbury steak for lunch.

In the afternoon, things aren't much better. Mrs. Eddy makes us write each of our spelling words ten times. In cursive. Even our extra-big bonus word: *mythological.* Plus, she reads a myth to us during snack time about a guy named Argus who had a hundred eyes all over his body. That might sound like an extra-good thing, but Jolene brought grapes to share. Eating grapes while listening to a story about a guy who has a hundred eyeballs is not the greatest. Trust me.

By the time recess rolls around, I've decided the mermaid has taken the day off. Just then, while everyone else is heading out the door, Stacey gives me a sly smile, gets up, and walks over to Mrs. Eddy, who is erasing the chalkboard.

"Mrs. Eddy?" Stacey says. "I have a question."

Mrs. Eddy sets down her eraser. "Yes?"

"Yesterday, when Mrs. Madson was here, she said she could use some help... um... cleaning the music room and...um...alphabetizing her songs. So I said I would love to help her. Plus, she told me I could bring along a friend."

"I see," Mrs. Eddy says.

"So I was wondering if Ida and I could help Mrs. Madson during our afternoon recess?"

Mrs. Eddy thinks for a moment. "I don't see why not," she says. "Let me double check with Mrs. Mad—"

"I just saw her on the way back from lunch," Stacey interrupts. "And she said today during recess would be *perfect*." Stacey gives Mrs. Eddy her biggest smile.

"Well, then," Mrs. Eddy says, smiling back. "It sounds like a fine plan."

Stacey grins at me as she clears off her desk.

I grin back even though alphabetizing and cleaning are not my best subjects.

"This is extra good, huh?" I say to Stacey as we head to the music room. "Even though Mrs. Madson *is* a little scary. And I hate cleaning, but I'm sure it will be fun to sweep with y—"

"Ida," Stacey interrupts. "We're not *really* going to help Mrs. Madson."

I stop. "We're not?"

41

"The mermaid just put that idea into my head so we can do something extra fun. Just the two of us!"

"Oh," I say, fidgeting a little.

Stacey pulls me along to the girls' bathroom. She checks all the stalls. "No one here!" she says, smiling.

I give her half a smile back and look around. Four stalls. Three sinks. One paper towel dispenser. "So what are we going to do?"

"Anything we want!" Stacey says, scooting up onto a sink and swinging her legs like she's sitting on the edge of a million possibilities.

I look around again trying to see things the way Stacey sees them. "I never noticed how much there isn't to do in here," I say.

"Yeah, but it's still fun not doing anything with your best friend!" Stacey replies.

"That's true," I say.

I walk over to one of the sinks and try to think of all the fun things it can do. I turn on the cold water faucet. Then I turn on the hot water faucet. Then I pump soap straight down the drain.

Stacey hops off her sink and turns on the water.

Then she turns on the water in the next sink, too. Pretty soon the whole place sounds like Niagara Falls.

A cumulus cloud of suds starts creeping up out of my drain. I pump in more soap and the suds cloud crawls right over the sides of the sink and plops onto the floor. "Hey, look!" I say to Stacey. "Suds-O-Rama!"

Stacey giggles and pumps soap into the other sinks. It isn't long before the floor is so foamy you'd swear we have a bad case of rabies or something.

A big glob of suds falls right onto Stacey's shoe. She does a fake scream. I fake-scream back. Each time a new glob falls, we fake-scream together. Again and again and again.

"*What* is going on in here?!" someone suddenly barks.

Stacey and I whip around.

Mrs. Madson is standing in the doorway of the girls' bathroom with a big frown on her face. Apparently, she doesn't realize what a fun place this is.

I quickly turn off the water in my sink. Stacey turns the water off in the other sinks. We stand

43

there staring at the foamy floor. The only sound I can hear is the popping of soap bubbles. And the tapping of Mrs. Madson's blood-red shoe.

"Um...we got dirty...playing dodgeball," Stacey says quickly. "And so our teacher told us to come in here and get cleaned up."

"I guess we got a little carried away," I add.

Mrs. Madson sucks in a long, deep breath. When she lets it out again I'm pretty sure I see flames flickering from her nose. "Clean. Up. This. *Mess.*"

I start cranking the paper towel machine like I'm an organ monkey. A moment later, I'm down on my hands and knees sopping up suds. So is Stacey.

"Go back to your classroom *immediately,*" Mrs. Madson says when the mess is gone. "The next time I catch you goofing around in here I will send you to Principal Stevens!"

"Thank you," I say.

We squeeze past Mrs. Madson and bolt out the door.

Everyone is back from recess when we get to the classroom.

"All done helping Mrs. Madson?" Mrs. Eddy asks as we zoom to our desks.

"Yes, we're very fast alphabetizers," Stacey says.

"Not to mention cleaners," I add.

I flip open my desk and take out a notebook and pencil.

I write *I will never goof around again* five times.

In cursive.

Chapter
5

"I'd rather touch worm guts than get caught goofing around again," I say to Stacey as we walk through the park on our way to the Purdee Good after school. "Maybe even *eat* them. Next time, let's ask the mermaid not to let us have *too* much fun."

Stacey laughs. "My dad says you can never have too much fun *or* too many friends."

My toe catches on a tree root and I stumble a little. "But one *best* friend is enough, right?"

Stacey smiles. "One best friend is plenty," she says. "But it doesn't hurt to have a few back-up friends, does it?"

"Back-up friends are okay," I say. "I like Randi and Meeka and Jolene. And even Brooke, when she isn't showing off her latest pageant crown."

"And even Jenna?" Stacey asks.

"Um...I like Jenna when she's out of town," I offer.

We walk out of the park and turn the corner on to Main Street, which leads right past Miss Woo's Dance Studio. The studio is on the first floor of an old brick building, and Miss Woo's apartment is on the second floor. Stacey says Miss Woo grew up, tragically, in a Chinese orphanage and then ran away to fulfill her dream of becoming a ballet dancer. I've never gotten around to telling Stacey I overheard Miss Woo say she was born and raised in Chicago.

I glance inside the big studio window and see Miss Woo standing on her tiptoes, only she's not dancing. She's reaching into a cabinet which is twice as tall as she is. She pulls out a small shoe box and carries it over to Jenna Drews, who is sitting on a bench taking off her regular shoes. Mr. Drews is there, too, holding a bright orange leotard with exploding fireworks on it. Rachel Drews and some other kindergarteners spin and skip across the big wooden floor.

"Speaking of ol' green braids," I say to Stacey,

pointing through the window at Jenna. I laugh. Stacey just smiles and keeps walking.

We cross the street to the Purdee Good Café. Stacey opens the jingly door and we walk inside. The Purdee Good used to be the kind of café my dad calls a *greasy spoon*. But last year Quinn Kloud's parents bought it and they don't believe in grease. Now there are bright blue curtains in the front windows and the walls are painted the color of cinnamon. The whole place smells like cinnamon, too. A big blackboard hangs over the counter and the daily menu is written on it with colored chalk. Even though most of the stuff they serve includes bean sprouts and organic mushrooms, I like coming here.

Stacey's mom is standing behind the counter, putting cookies into a glass display case. There's a name tag on her shirt that says, HI! I'M YOUR PURDEE GOOD SERVER: KELLI.

Kelli looks up at us and smiles. She has the exact same smile Stacey has. In fact, she pretty much has the same face as Stacey. Only her eyes are blue instead of brown. And her hair is blond and spiky like the top of a lemon meringue pie.

Stacey's hair is longer and darker and curlier. Maybe Stacey got her dark eyes and hair from her dad. I don't know because I've never met him.

"Hi, guys!" Kelli calls to us.

"Hi, Kelli!" we call back.

"The usual?" she asks, holding up a giant chocolate-chip cookie.

We nod and walk over to the counter while Kelli puts the cookie on a plate. She slides it toward us. "How was school?" she asks.

"Oh, you know," I say. "The usual."

Kelli smiles at me. Then she turns to Stacey. "What about the math quiz you missed yesterday? Did you have it today?"

"Yep," Stacey says. "I think I got a perfect score."

"That's my girl!" Kelli says, giving Stacey's arm a squeeze. "I'll get you two some milk to go with the cookie."

As soon as Kelli's busy with the milk, I turn to Stacey. "Why did you do that?" I whisper.

"Do what?" Stacey whispers back.

"Lie about taking the math quiz today."

"Oh, that," Stacey says. "Well, I couldn't tell her the real reason we didn't have it. I mean, she would never believe that an evil mermaid put a spell on it."

"You could have said it's still canceled without explaining why," I say.

"But then she would have made me study for it again tonight." Stacey slides the cookie toward me. "You break, I choose," she says.

I pick up the cookie and break it in half. Stacey chooses the half she wants and I take the other. "Still," I say, "what if the spell wears off and we really do have to take the quiz and you get a lot wrong?"

Stacey gives me a patient smile. "Relax, Ida," she says. "Kelli won't remember any of this by tomorrow. She's got more important stuff to think about."

I'm just about to ask what kind of stuff when Kelli returns with our milk. "I have to work late tonight, Stace," she says, "but Grandma will be home."

Stacey nods.

"Oh, and Ida, your mom called a little while

ago," Kelli says to me. "She wanted to remind you that she'll pick you up in a few minutes. Something about a haircut?"

I sigh. "Oh, yeah," I say. "I forgot. It's just a trim."

Stacey picks up her glass of milk. "Let's sit at a booth until your mom comes, okay, Ida?" she says.

I follow Stacey to a booth near the back of the café. We slip off our backpacks and sit down across from each other. Stacey taps her cookie on the edge of her glass and says, "I call this meeting of The Secret Mermaid Club to order."

"Here, here," I reply, tapping my cookie on the table. I pull the mermaid out of my backpack and set her behind the napkin container so she's mostly hidden. "Let's do our club pledge."

We put our hands on top of the mermaid. "I solemnly swear to light this mermaid every night no matter how much the sight of her evil, glowing grin makes me want to pee my pants," we say together.

We lean back in the booth and work on our milk and cookies. "Now what?" I ask.

"Now we discuss today's spell," Stacey says. "I think it went well, don't you?"

I practically choke on my cookie. "Went *well*? We almost got sent to the principal's office!"

"That's only because the mermaid is still getting warmed up," Stacey says. "The more we use her, the stronger she'll get. That's why we should ask for another spell right away so she gets more practice."

"Okay," I say. "But if it involves a paper towel dispenser, I'm out."

Stacey smiles. "It should involve just the two of us doing something fun." She looks around the café, thinking. I look around, too. Kelli is putting away dishes behind the counter. A man wearing a suit is sitting at a table, reading a newspaper. The door jingles and two older ladies walk in, laughing and talking. They sit at the counter and Kelli sets two coffee cups in front of them.

"Kelli told me some people come in here every day," Stacey says.

"That works for me," I say, taking a bite out of my cookie. "Only let's skip the coffee part."

"It doesn't work for me," Stacey says. "Not when I have to go to my dad's." Stacey's quiet for a moment and then she gets her far-off look. "Unless . . . ," she says.

"Unless what?"

Stacey looks at me. "Unless that's our next spell."

"Huh?"

Stacey leans in. "Ida," she whispers. "Can I spend the weekend at your house?"

"Um . . . of course, but . . . don't you have to . . ."

"Good!" Stacey cuts in. "Because I want to spend the weekend at your house, too. *This* weekend."

Stacey puts her hand on the mermaid and scrunches up her eyes like she's trying to bend a spoon with her mind. "Dear Mermaid," she whispers. "Make it so I don't have to go to my dad's this weekend. Make it so I can spend the weekend with Ida!"

Stacey opens her eyes again and looks at the mermaid.

I look at her, too. "Are you sure the mermaid is powerful enough to do something like *that*?"

Stacey thinks for a moment. "Yes," she replies. "If we help her a little."

"Help her?"

Stacey leans in again. "Here's what we'll do. First, ask your mom if I can spend the weekend with you. Tell her Kelli will be working and my grandma will be...um...at a bowling tournament."

"I didn't know your grandma was a bowler," I say.

"She's not," Stacey replies. "It will make the story more...interesting."

"But...isn't that...lying?"

Stacey thinks for a moment. "It's more like... *imagining.*"

"Um—"

"Then after school on Friday," Stacey continues, "I'll call my dad and tell him I'm sick and need to stay home with Kelli. Then I'll tell Kelli that my dad called to say he has to go out of town for work and won't be back until Monday. Then I'll ask her if I can spend the weekend with you instead! I know she'll say yes."

Stacey gives me a big smile.

I tap my cookie on the table and fidget a little. "It sounds sort of...complicated," I say.

"Don't worry, Ida," Stacey replies. "The mermaid will take care of the complicated stuff."

Stacey keeps going over the plan again and again and I keep nodding like it all makes a lot of sense. But inside I'm wishing I could draw it out in my sketchbook like a comic strip. Then I could see the beginning, middle, and end all at once, like Stacey can. Then maybe it would feel more like a story than a lie.

"Ask your mom tonight," Stacey says. "And tell me what she says tomorrow."

The door jingles and my eyes dart up, expecting to see my mom walking in.

But it's not my mom.

It's Jenna Drews.

Chapter

6

Jenna walks into the Purdee Good with her dad. I grab the mermaid and stick her back inside my backpack just as Jenna zeroes in on us.

"Hi, Stacey!" she calls from across the café. A moment later her green braids are bobbing over to our booth. I dunk my cookie in my milk and watch it turn to mush.

"Hi, Jenna!" Stacey says back. "Do you want to sit with us?"

"Of course," Jenna says, scooting in next to Stacey. "I just got done shopping."

"What for?" I mumble. "New hair?"

"New *ballet shoes*," Jenna says. "*All* my shoes are getting too small." She lifts her foot and wags it around. "I'm a size *six* now. In *women's*."

I tuck my size-four feet under the booth bench and take a bite out of my soggy cookie.

"I got my dad to buy me a new leotard, too," Jenna continues. "It's orange with fireworks. You'll love it, Stacey."

"I can't wait to see it!" Stacey replies.

"I'll wear it to dance on Thursday," Jenna says. "Unless you want to see it now. It's in my car. Let's—"

"She can't," I interrupt.

Jenna whips a look at me. "Why not?"

"Because we're in the middle of ... something," I say.

"What?" Jenna asks.

"Um ... nothing," I mumble.

"We were just talking about our new clu—," Stacey starts to say.

I give her a kick.

"Ouch!"

"Sorry," I say. "My feet must be getting too big for this booth."

"Your new *club*?" Jenna asks.

Stacey rubs her shin, and gives Jenna a nod.

I give Stacey a very serious look. Then I turn to Jenna. "What Stacey means is we were talking about how *stupid* clubs are. And ... um ... how we would never want to start one."

"Oh . . . r-right," Stacey says. "I forgot. I mean, yes, that's what we were talking about."

Jenna lifts her chin. "I belong to *three* clubs," she says. "And none of them are stupid. My mother says clubs build character, confidence, and creativity."

"Brought to you by the letter C," I mumble.

Just then Mr. Drews walks up to our booth carrying a take-n-bake pizza. "Time to go, Jenna," he says.

"I just got here!" Jenna says back.

"No time to argue, kiddo," Mr. Drews says. "I need to drop off some paperwork with our insurance guy, pick up Rachel from dance, and then get Jade. She's babysitting while Mom and I are at a meeting tonight." Jade is Brooke Morgan's older sister. She babysits for half the kids in town.

"*Another* meeting?" Jenna says.

"Yep," Mr. Drews replies, shifting the pizza. "It's a busy time for meetings. C'mon, let's go!"

"I want to show Stacey my new leotard," Jenna grumbles.

"Show her at dance class," Mr. Drews replies.

"I want to show her *now*!" Jenna snaps.

Mr. Drews sighs. "Fine," he says. "Stacey, why don't you ask your mom if you can come over, and then I'll take you home after our meeting."

Jenna grins.

"What about Ida?" Stacey asks.

"Yes, of course, Ida, too," Mr. Drews says, checking his watch.

"I can't," I mumble. "I have to get my hair trimmed."

"Oh, well," Jenna says. "Too bad." She slides out of the booth.

Mr. Drews hands the pizza to Jenna and pulls a thick envelope from his back pocket. "Take the pizza to the car while I run these papers next door," he says to Jenna. "Then I'll get Rachel." A moment later he's heading down the sidewalk.

"Tell your mom, Stacey," Jenna says, "then meet me outside." She marches out the door with the pizza.

"I'm sorry, Ida. I don't know what just happened!" Stacey says.

"You *told* her," I say. "About our club!"

"I know," Stacey says. "But I didn't tell her much."

"It was enough!"

"Don't worry, Ida," Stacey says. "Jenna will be so busy talking about dance, she'll forget all about the club." She snags her backpack and slips out of the booth.

I just shake my head. "I've known Jenna for a long time," I say. "She never forgets anything."

The door jingles again and my mom walks in. She gives me a wave and then starts talking to Kelli.

"I better go," Stacey says. "Don't forget to ask your mom about this weekend. Oh, and be sure to plug in the mermaid early tonight. She's going to need extra power to make our plan happen!"

I nod.

"Great!" Stacey says, smiling. "See you tomorrow, Ida!"

"Great," I say back. "See you tomorrow."

Chapter
7

Even though I plan to ask my mom right away if Stacey can spend the weekend with us, I don't. Part of me decides it's a bad idea to ask her at the Purdee Good, in case she mentions the plan to Kelli. Another part of me decides it's not a good idea to ask her while I'm getting my hair trimmed in case I fidget and end up with crooked bangs. And by the time we're driving home, a third part of me decides it will be better to ask her after I figure out exactly what I'm going to say.

When we get home I go straight to my bedroom. I pull off my backpack and drop it on the floor. The mermaid clunks inside.

"George," I say, turning to my bed. "I need to practice something on you."

George gives me his *this-can't-be-good* look.

I pick up George and set him on my desk chair. I put his monkey paws on the edge of my desk, like he's playing a piano. "Pretend you're Mom," I tell him. "Play something hard so you're only half listening."

I study George's paws and imagine I hear music coming out of my desk.

"Hi, Mom," I say, giving George a wave. "I'm sorry to interrupt your practicing, but I have a very small question to ask you that only requires a quick answer, such as yes."

I pause. George shifts a little on the chair.

"Stacey's mom has to work this weekend and her grandmother is going to be...um...elsewhere. So we thought—I mean...*I* thought—it would make a lot of sense if Stacey stayed with us. For the weekend. Which would be very helpful to everyone involved."

I pause for a moment, thinking. Then I cup my hand around George's ear. "Ask if it's okay with Stacey's mom," I whisper to him.

I listen for a moment and then I do a very casual laugh. "Well, of course it's probably okay with her. I mean, they see each other every day and so it for sure must have come up in their conversation. Probably several times." I do the laugh again.

One of George's paws slips off the desk. I put it back. He gives me a look that I wasn't expecting.

"Um...yes...I think it's okay with Stacey's dad," I say. "I mean, I *know* it is because he wants Stacey to make lots of friends and so he will be happy if she skips a weekend with him to stay with me."

I gulp. "I mean...what I *meant* to say was..."

George's paw slips off my desk again. A moment later the rest of him slips off my chair and clunks to the floor.

I sigh and clunk to the floor, too.

Later, when my dad comes into my room to say good night, I'm ready. That's because when I plugged in the mermaid, she gave me the idea to ask *him* if Stacey can spend the weekend because he's much better at saying yes quickly than my mom is. Plus, he can tell my mom all about the plan and that will save me a lot of time.

I have the covers pulled up over my head when my dad sits down next to me.

"All ready for bed?" he asks.

"Mmm-hmm," I say from under my covers.

I hear him smile. "Need anything? Extra blanket? Glass of water? Oxygen?"

"Nope, I'm good," I say, even though a little air would be nice.

"Well, then, good night, Ida." He leans in to kiss the top of my covered head.

"Good night," I say back. "Oh, and Dad?"

"Yes?"

"I was just wondering if it would be okay...I mean...I think it would be a good idea if...if Stacey...if she..."

"If she what?" Dad asks, pulling back my covers so he can see a corner of my face.

"If Stacey spends the weekend with us?"

"Oh," Dad says. He thinks for a moment. "I don't see why not, but you better check with Mom."

"I was thinking maybe *you* could check with her for me."

My dad leans in again and kisses the part of me he can see. "Better ask her yourself so you can work out the details," he says. "Sound good?"

I sigh. "Sounds good," I reply.

My dad gets up to leave, but then he stops. "Huh," he says, looking at the mermaid. "I thought Mom threw that night-light out years ago."

I sit up a little. "Why would she throw it out?"

"I bought it when you were two," he says. "You cried every time we plugged it in." He picks up the mermaid and studies her glowing grin. "Now I remember why."

He sets the mermaid down and heads for the door. "Sleep tight, Ida," he says.

"I'll try," I reply, glancing at the mermaid and ducking under my covers.

The next morning, I come up with a third plan.

In this plan, I write a *note* to my mom explaining the whole Stacey situation.

Dear Mom,

How are you? I am fine. Oh, by the way, I think it would be a good idea for Stacey to spend the weekend with us. Her mom will be busy working. And her grandmother has other requirements. Also, we could do our homework, which would be educational.

Yours truly,
Ida May

P.S. In addition, it will keep me out of your hair.

I read the note and smile. Then I pick up my backpack and walk downstairs to the piano. I set the note on the middle C key. Then I holler good-bye to my mom and hurry out the door.

Chapter

8

Thankfully, Jenna isn't at the bus stop so I don't have to hear her brag about all the fun she had with Stacey yesterday.

As soon as I get to school I go to the broken water fountain and wait for Stacey. It isn't long before I see her coming down the hallway. She's wearing a big smile. And a pair of springy star antennae on top of her head.

I grin as Stacey walks up to me. "Where'd you get those?" I ask, pointing at the springy stars.

"From Grandma Tootie!" Stacey replies. She jiggles her head and the stars make wild orbits over her. "Actually, technically, I got them from the mermaid."

"The *mermaid*?"

Stacey nods and the stars bow. "After I got

home from Jenna's house I asked the mermaid to make something fun happen."

"Because you didn't have any fun at Jenna's house, right?"

"No, we had fun," Stacey says.

"Oh," I say back.

"I wanted something *extra* fun!"

"But the mermaid was with me, so how—," I start to say.

"All I had to do was think it, and she made it happen!"

"Wow," I say. "She really is getting more powerful."

Stacey nods again. "I have a pair for you, too!" She pulls another headband out of her backpack and holds it out to me. Even though springy stars are sort of second grade, I put them on because when your best friend is wearing a pair, you want to wear a pair, too.

I jiggle my head and the stars send springy signals to my brain, which loosens up my good news. "Guess what?" I say.

"What?" Stacey says back.

"Last night, I asked my dad if you can spend the weekend and he said it's okay with him!"

Stacey does an excited little jump, which makes her stars go crazy. "Your mom said it's okay, too, right?" she asks. She gives me a big, hopeful smile.

I think about the note I left on the piano. "Of course," I say. "She's completely in favor of the whole plan."

Stacey does the little jump again and I do the little jump, too, because it's easier to believe anything is true if you are jumping with your best friend.

We link arms and bob down the hallway together. As soon as we turn the corner to our classroom I stop bobbing. "Uh-oh," I say.

Stacey stops, too. "What's wrong?" she asks.

I point down the hallway. "Henna Jenna. She's up to something."

Jenna is standing outside our classroom, holding a lumpy plastic bag and talking with the other girls from our class—Meeka, Jolene, Randi, and Brooke.

Stacey studies Jenna's bag. She shrugs. "Maybe she brought brownies for the class," she offers.

"In a *bag*?" I shake my head. "It's something else."

"Well, there's only one way to find out," Stacey says, pulling on my arm.

I pull back. "Let's not," I say. "Let's . . . find another way to the classroom. A *secret* way."

Stacey raises her eyebrows. "Ida, our classroom is at the end of the hall. There's no other way to get there except *this* way!" She starts tugging on my arm again.

"We could go outside and . . . and . . ."

"And what? Climb in a window?"

"Okay," I say.

Stacey laughs and her stars clap like baby hands.

I sigh. "I know climbing in the window isn't going to work unless the mermaid gives us wings like the goddess Nike. But if we go down there, Jenna will suck us into whatever's inside that bag."

Stacey takes my arm and pulls me toward Jenna and the other girls. "Don't worry, Ida," she says. "The mermaid will take care of everything."

Halfway down the hall, I see Jenna taking T-shirts out of the lumpy plastic bag and handing them to the other girls. They slip them on over their regular shirts. Each shirt has DO-GOOD NYMPHS written on it in big swirly letters. There's

70

also a drawing of a girl with pointy ears and leaves stuck in her long wavy hair. It's a good drawing, but it still feels like bad news to me.

Jenna pulls out another shirt and lets the bag float to the floor. I see she's wearing one of the shirts, too. "Hi, Stacey!" she calls to us. "Congratulations! You're the newest member of the Do-Good Nymphs!"

"The *Who*-good *what*?" I ask, walking up to the group with Stacey.

"The *Do*-Good *Nymphs*," Jenna says back. "My new *club*." She holds the shirt out to Stacey. "Put it on!"

Stacey takes off her backpack and springy stars. She sets them down and slips on the shirt.

"What's a nymph?" Brooke asks, studying the drawing on everyone's shirt. Except mine.

Jenna gives Brooke a look. "Don't you listen when Mr. Crow reads us myths?"

"Yes," Brooke replies. "What's a nymph?"

Jenna rolls her eyes. "Nymphs are biological creatures that the gods invented."

"Don't you mean *myth*ological creatures?" I ask.

Jenna darts a look at me. "That, too."

"Like fairies?" Jolene asks.

"And mermaids?" Meeka adds.

I feel a zing in my brain when Meeka mentions *mermaids,* but I don't think it's from my springy stars.

"They're *better* than fairies and mermaids," Jenna says. "*Tougher.* They take care of trees and rivers and stuff. *And* they do good deeds to people. In my club, any nymph who does a good deed gets a reward."

"What kind of reward?" Jolene asks.

Jenna lifts her chin and grins. "A leaf," she replies.

"A *leaf*?" we all say together.

Jenna nods. "The nymph who collects the most leaves wins a prize."

Brooke's eyes go glinty, like a crow's. "What kind of prize?" she asks.

"A special one," Jenna says. "I'll decide."

Everyone starts talking at once about the new club. Jenna listens and smiles.

I think about yesterday when Jenna showed up at the Purdee Good during our secret mermaid meeting.

I give Jenna a squint. "How did you get the idea to start a new *club*?" I ask.

Jenna glances at me. "I'm always coming up with new ideas," she says. Then she turns to the others. "So, how do you like your club shirts?" she asks. "I made my mom go out and buy them last night after she got home from ... after she got home. I had to stay up until ten making them."

Stacey glances at me. "Ida, put your nymph shirt on!"

I look at the empty bag lying on the floor. "Um ... there seems to be a shortage," I reply.

Stacey looks at the bag, too. Then she looks at Jenna. "Where's Ida's shirt?" she asks.

Jenna shrugs. "They came three to a package and my mom only bought two packages."

"Didn't you tell her you needed *seven* shirts?" Stacey asks.

Jenna flicks her green braids off her sharp shoulders. "Maybe it was too late to go back and get another one, okay?" she snaps. "Besides, Ida probably doesn't even want to be in my club. She's always saying clubs are stupid."

Everyone looks at me, waiting for an answer.

I don't say anything. I just stand there, wishing I wasn't the only one still wearing springy stars on top of my head.

"Well, if Ida isn't in the club then I'm not either," Stacey says. She starts to pull off her nymph shirt. So does Randi. Then Brooke. Then Meeka and Jolene.

Jenna's hands shoot up like a school crossing guard. "Keep your shirts on!" she shouts.

Everyone freezes.

Jenna crosses her arms and taps the toe of her clog. Then she peels off *her* nymph shirt and shoves it at me. "I'll make another one tonight," she says. "It should be different, anyway, since I'm the club leader."

The bell rings and Jenna kicks the empty bag out of the way. She starts herding all the Do-Good Nymphs into the classroom. Stacey picks up her stuff and glances back at me. "Coming, Ida?" she asks.

"In a minute," I say, holding up the shirt Jenna jammed into my hands. "I want to put this on first."

Stacey nods and lets Jenna yank her inside.

As soon as everyone's gone, I open my back-pack and find a black marker—the smelly kind that doesn't wash off. I lay the shirt on the floor and study the nymph.

I give her a few fangs.

And one capital *V* eyebrow.

And several spiders in her long, wavy hair.

Then I change the swirly *D* in *Do* to an *N*.

I take off my springy stars and pull the shirt on.

I read myself and grin.

9

When I get inside the classroom the first thing I notice is Mr. Crow. He's sitting at his desk looking a lot less green than the last time I saw him.

"Hi, Mr. Crow," I say. "Are you feeling better?"

"Much better. Thanks, Ida," he says back. "It sounds like Mrs. Eddy handled things while I was gone?"

I nod. "She read some more myths to us. She even told us about her favorite one."

"Which one?" Mr. Crow asks.

"The one about Zeus and how he almost got eaten by his father, just like most of his unfortunate brothers and sisters. But then Zeus's grandmother hid him in a cave until he was old enough to stand up to his father and make him cough up the other kids."

Mr. Crow smiles. "That's one of my favorite myths, too," he says. "Did Mrs. Eddy mention where the cave was located?"

I think for a moment. "Nope," I say. "She only mentioned that Zeus's grandmother was Gaia, goddess of the Earth, which made Jenna's day."

Mr. Crow leans back in his chair and grins. "The cave was located on a mountain called Mount *Ida*," he says.

I give Mr. Crow a very serious squint. "You're kidding, right?"

"Nope," Mr. Crow says. "You share a name with a famous Greek landmark!"

"Who's Ida named after?" I hear someone say.

I turn and see one of the Dylans walking up to Mr. Crow with a note in his hand.

Mr. Crow takes the note and says, "Not *who*. *What*. Mount Ida is a famous mountain on the island of Crete."

"Cool!" Dylan says.

"What's cool?" Randi asks on her way to the pencil sharpener.

"Ida's named after a famous Greek mountain!" Dylan says.

"Actually, I'm named after my grandmother," I mumble. "Only she's not famous. I don't even think she's Greek."

Randi snorts. "At least you're not named after a restaurant," she says.

"You're named after a *restaurant*?" Dylan asks.

"Yep," Randi replies. "RANDI'S RESTAURANT. HOME OF THE WORLD FAMOUS PIG SKIN FRIES. I popped out under the neon sign. My dad figured they should either name me Randi or Pig Skin. My mom went with Randi."

"Wow," Dylan says, all impressed. "I wish I was named after something famous."

"There's a famous singer named Bob Dylan," Mr. Crow offers.

"A *singer*?" Dylan says. "Isn't there a volcano or a ditch or something named Dylan?"

"Not that I know of," Mr. Crow replies.

Dylan sighs and trudges to his desk.

Randi heads to the pencil sharpener.

I turn toward my desk, but before I can take a step Jenna is in my face. "Excuse me, Mount Ida," she says. "The Do-Good Nymphs are meeting during recess." She pushes a piece of notebook paper at me. I take it and see a nymph drawn at the top, just like the one that used to be on my T-shirt.

Do-Good Nymphs Meeting
WHEN: Today (at recess)
WHERE: In the Pigpen
WHO: ALL nymphs
(Attendance is required!!)

Jenna turns away, but as she does she glances at my shirt. "How come your nymph has *fangs?*" she asks. "And *spiders?*"

I glance down at my shirt. Then I glance up at Jenna. "Marker malfunction?"

Jenna huffs and stomps away.

Later, when it's time for recess, Jenna grabs a clipboard from her desk and we all head to a circle of hedges on the playground that our custodian, Mr. Benson, trimmed to look like hogs. Joey started calling the space in the middle of the hedgehogs the pigpen. Get it? Now everyone calls it that.

We all sit in a circle on the grass. Except for

Brooke, who doesn't believe in sitting on grass. And Jenna, who doesn't believe in circles.

"First, I'll read my club rules," Jenna announces.

"*Rules?*" we all groan.

Jenna nods. "Every club needs rules," she says. "That's a rule." She starts reading from her clipboard.

"Rule #1: Attendance is required at all meetings."

"So far, so good," I mumble.

"Rule #2: "Nymphs must do good deeds to earn leaves."

Randi reaches over and smashes a bug that's crawling across Brooke's shoe. Brooke yelps like a small dog and practically jumps over a hedgehog. Randi holds up her buggy hand. "Gimme a leaf," she says.

All Jenna gives Randi is a look. "Rule #3: Nymphs do not *destroy* nature."

Randi wipes her hand on the grass, grinning.

"Rule #4: The nymph that does the most good deeds earns a special prize."

"What kind of prize?" Brooke asks. Her eyes go all glinty again.

"I already told you, Brooke," Jenna says. "I'll decide. The one who deserves it the most will get it at our next meeting."

"When's that?" Meeka asks.

"Tomorrow, right after dance," Jenna says.

"I don't go to dance," Randi says.

"Me, neither," I add.

Jenna does an impatient sigh. "Then you'll just have to wait for us at the park," Jenna says to me and Randi.

Jenna clips her pen to her clipboard. "Now it's time to patrol the playground."

"Huh?" we all chime in.

"Do-good nymphs make sure everyone is following the rules and no one is hurting nature." She shoots a look at Randi.

Jenna herds us out of the pigpen. We follow her around the playground looking for first graders who are tangled in swing chains, and second graders who need a lecture about sharing jump ropes, and third graders who are tearing wings off flies.

Just as the bell rings, Jenna sees Joey and Dominic trying to karate chop a stick in half. "Break that stick and I break your necks!" Jenna shouts from across the playground.

Joey and Dominic drop the stick and run inside.

When we get back to our classroom it's time to practice our spelling words. But my brain is so nymphalized, I leave the *H* off *honesty* and give *confront* two *U*s.

After Mr. Crow has us chant out our extra-big bonus word ("MYTH!...O!...LOG!...I!...CAL!"), Jenna just can't help herself. She jumps up and tells all about her new club. She even makes me, Stacey, Brooke, Randi, Meeka, and Jolene stand up and model our new club shirts.

"Maybe the Do-Good Nymphs would like to plan a presentation for our Greek Day parents' program?" Mr. Crow suggests.

Jenna's green braids practically start clapping. "Of course!" she says.

Mr. Crow gives Jenna a smile. "In fact, everyone needs to start planning their presentations. It's only a couple weeks away."

"What kind of presentation?" Tom asks.

"Anything you want," Mr. Crow says. "Sing a song, do a skit, read a poem—anything that has to do with a Greek myth."

Jenna's hand shoots up. "What about a dance?" she asks.

"A dance would be great!" Mr. Crow replies.

Jenna yanks her clipboard out of her desk and starts writing.

When I get home after school, my mom is sitting at the kitchen table going through a stack of mail.

"Hi, Ida!" she says, glancing up at me. "How was school?"

"Oh, you know," I say. "The usual."

She gives me a smile. Then she reads my shirt. "The No-Good Nymphs?" she asks.

"It's a new club Jenna started," I say. "We had our first meeting today and we have another one after school tomorrow so I'll be getting home a little late."

"A new club sounds like fun," Mom says.

"Some are," I say back.

I fish around in the stack of mail. "Um... did you get any... notes today?"

"Nope, just bills," Mom says, tearing open an envelope.

"No, I mean *notes*. The kind that come on scraps of paper."

Mom thinks for a moment. "I don't remember getting any notes," she says. "Why? Did you leave one?"

I fidget a little. "I might have," I say. "On the piano. Didn't you see it?"

"No," she says, getting up from the table. "I don't give piano lessons on Wednesdays. I'll read it right now."

"Um...maybe it would be better if..."

Before my brain can churn up a reason why she should skip reading the note until I have time to practice answering any questions that might come up, she takes off for the piano, finds the note, and reads it on her way back to me.

"You want Stacey to spend the weekend?" she asks, looking up from the note.

I nod.

"Did Stacey ask her mom?"

I nod again.

"And it's okay with her dad?"

I nod a third time.

"Well, then, it sounds like a great plan." She

tosses the note onto the table. "Get washed up and then you can help me start supper, okay?"

I nod a fourth time and hurry to the bathroom. I close the door behind me and do an extra-big sigh of relief because nodding doesn't require any imagining at all.

I walk over to the sink and turn on the water. I pump soap into my hand. Then I start scrubbing. Suds and germs plop into the sink and slide down the drain. I scrub my arms, too. And clip my nails.

Then I go back to the kitchen feeling very clean.

After supper, I call Stacey. "Guess what?" I say. "It's for extra sure now. You can spend the weekend with me."

Stacey does an excited little squeal. "Guess what else? My dad called earlier and while we were talking I remembered to cough twice and sneeze three times. When he asked if I was catching a cold I said, 'I think maybe I am,' and then he said, 'I hope you're feeling better by the weekend,' and I said, 'Oh, I'm sure I will be,' and then I sneezed *again*. So now when I call him on Friday to say that I'm sick it won't sound made up at all!"

"Wow," I say. "You are so good at...um... imagining."

"It's easier now that the mermaid is putting ideas into my head," Stacey says. "I can't wait for the weekend!"

"I can't wait, too," I say back. "Just you and me!"

"And the mermaid!" Stacey adds.

Chapter
10

The next morning, I get to the bus stop extra early so my mom won't be tempted to start a long conversation about my weekend plans with Stacey. The first person to show up is Rachel.

"Where's Jenna?" I ask.

"She's running a little late," Rachel says. She holds up her wrist so I can see her frog watch. The frog's tongue ticks off the seconds. "My dad got it for me last night at Buzz's Bait Shop. We needed groceries."

"They sell groceries at Buzz's Bait Shop?" I ask.

Rachel nods. "Milk and eggs and wax worms," she says. "Only they keep that stuff in the cooler, not the bargain bin. That's where he found my new watch and Jenna's new shirt."

Rachel checks her frog again. "She should be here in seven," she says.

I nod and notice Quinn and Tess coming around the corner toward us.

"Yes, it's a busy time in my family," Rachel continues. She pulls a red crayon and a pad of yellow sticky notes from her pocket. "Busy, busy, busy." She writes scribbles and numbers on the pad. Then she pulls off the note and hands it to me.

"What's this for?" I ask, taking the note from her and studying the scribbles.

"If you need to reach me," she says.

"Um...okay," I say and stick the note to my sleeve.

Rachel gives me a nod. "I need you to be a good helper until things get back to normal," she adds.

"Um...okay," I say again.

Then Rachel starts in on another note. More scribbles and a few letters. She's still too little to write real words.

As soon as Quinn and Tess get to the bus stop Rachel holds the sticky note out to Tess. "In case of emergency," she says.

Tess frowns at the scribbles. "No, thank you," she replies.

Rachel frowns back. "I don't want to hear another word!" she shouts and jabs the note at Tess.

Tess takes it and sticks it to her shoe.

Rachel makes her face go soft. She pats Tess's shoulder. "I'm sorry I yelled. I've just been so tired lately."

I glance up and see our bus coming around the corner.

I look down the street, but there's still no sign of Jenna.

Rachel looks, too. "Her meeting probably went longer than expected," she says. She bites her bottom lip and shifts a little in her shoes.

Just as the bus slows to a stop, I see Jenna running down the sidewalk toward us.

The doors open, but Rachel doesn't budge. Quinn pulls Tess past her and they climb on.

"You get on," I tell Rachel. "I won't let the bus leave without Jenna."

Rachel looks up at me. Then she climbs onto the bus. She stops at the top of the stairs, scribbles another note, and hands it to the bus driver. "I would appreciate a little more cooperation," she says.

"I'll keep that in mind," the driver replies, stuffing the note into her pocket.

I glance down the street again. Jenna is getting closer. Red face. Green braids flying.

"Will you be joining us today?" the bus driver calls down to me.

I glance up at her. "Um...yes. It's just that Jenna is running...a little late."

The driver glances down the street and sees Jenna. She toots the bus horn, like that is going to help the situation.

I keep waiting at the bottom of the steps until, finally, Jenna runs up behind me, breathing hard. Her braids look fuzzier than usual. Like she wore them to bed last night and then her mom didn't have time to rebraid them this morning. She's also wearing a new T-shirt. I know it's new because there's still a sticker on the sleeve that says CLEARANCE: $4.99. There's a nymph drawn on the shirt, but it's small and off to one side because most of the shirt is filled up by a big, puffy fish. NOW THAT'S A BIG FISH STORY! is printed under the fish in letters that look like fishhooks.

"Nice...um...shirt," I say.

Jenna just pushes past me and climbs onto the bus.

Our bus gets to school later than usual, so there isn't time to meet Stacey at the broken water fountain. And I don't get to spend any recess time with just her because Jenna keeps a tight leash on the nymphs all day, reminding us to do good deeds and promising a special prize at our meeting after dance today.

During cleanup at the end of the day, Mr. Crow lets all the dancers go to the bathroom and change into their dance clothes. That includes all of the girls, except me and Randi. And none of the boys, except Tom Sanders.

When the girls get back, everyone looks different. Brooke has her long hair bunched up in a pink scrunchy and she's wearing a pink leotard and pink warm-up pants. Meeka and Jolene have matching ponytails, sparkly purple leotards, and purple warm-up pants. Jenna has pinned her green braids to the top of her head. Her new orange leotard with the exploding fireworks peeks out from under her hoodie. Stacey's curly hair looks just the same, but she's wearing a black leotard and matching pants.

When the last bell rings, Jenna gets us all organized for the walk to Miss Woo's. She must have her good-deed radar turned up full blast because she marches ahead of the pack, picking up candy wrappers, rescuing a ball from a prickly bush for a little kid, and helping Mrs. Eddy walk across Birch Street.

"I'm quite capable of crossing the street by myself," Mrs. Eddy tells Jenna.

"I'm happy to help," Jenna replies, pulling her along.

When we get to the park, Randi takes off for the basketball court. "Holler when it's nymph time!" she yells as she dribbles away. I stop by a bench near the playground. "I'll wait for you guys here," I say.

Stacey stops, too. "Why don't you come with and watch us dance?" she asks.

I think about sitting at Miss Woo's watching Stacey and the other girls dance. I think about them twirling and pointing and pliéing around. Then I think about them whispering and giggling between dances and Stacey telling me later what they were whispering and giggling about, only it won't seem so funny the second time around.

I sit down on the bench. "I'm good," I say. "I want to work on a new drawing anyway." I slip off my backpack, unzip it, and pull out my sketchbook and a pencil.

Stacey gives me a smile. "Okay," she says. "We'll be back before you know it!" Then she hurries to catch up with the others.

"I'll be waiting," I say.

I look around the playground for something good to draw. Some little kids are getting pushed on the swings. Bigger kids dangle from the monkey bars. Several moms are talking at a picnic table while their babies swap soggy Cheerios from their strollers. Randi shoots hoops with some sixth graders on the basketball court. A squirrel darts in and out of a nearby bush.

"Will you watch this for me?" I hear someone say.

I look up and see a girl standing next to me. She pulls a wad of purple gum out of her mouth.

"Huh?" I say.

"We're not allowed to chew gum on the playground," she says, pointing to a sign that reads, NO GUM, DOGS, OR ROLLERBLADES ON THE EQUIPMENT. She sticks the gum on the bench next to me. "Thanks," she says and runs off. A moment later she's hanging upside down from the monkey bars.

The squirrel reappears with half a granola bar in its mouth.

"Friend of Jenna's?" I ask.

The squirrel doesn't answer. It just flicks its fluffy tail into a question mark and watches me with one beady eye. Then it takes the granola bar in its tiny doll hands and bites off the edges with its sharp, pointy teeth.

I glance at my muddy sneakers, which are just one shade away from a granola bar. I pull my feet up onto the bench, check on the gum, and start drawing.

First, I draw a face with beady eyes and sharp, pointy teeth. I give it fuzzy braids. And a furry body with a fluffy tail. I dress it in a fish shirt. And size six sneakers.

It's good, but it's just my warm-up drawing.

On the other side of the page I draw a girl with curly hair and dark eyes and no sharp teeth at all. I give her feathery arms, like bird wings, and long legs that could kick her to the sky.

"Thanks," I hear someone say.

I look up and see gum girl standing next to me. She pulls her purple wad off the bench and pops it back into her mouth.

"You're welcome," I reply.

"Who's that?" she asks, snooping at my

sketchbook.

"My best friend," I say, looking at my drawing of Stacey.

"Which one?" she asks. "The one with braids or the one with curls?"

"The one with *curls*," I say, pointing.

"Then who's the one with braids?" she asks.

"That's...someone else," I say.

"Not your friend?"

"Not exactly," I reply, checking my watch.

Gum girl studies the drawings some more. "You did that one better," she says, poking the page with her sticky finger.

She skips away.

I look at the page.

And see a purple smudge on a fuzzy braid.

Chapter 11

The squirrel has finished its granola bar and moved on to soggy Cheerios by the time the dancers get back. Randi sees them coming and catches up. Meeka and Jolene do a little hop-skip-jump together as they come down the path toward me. Brooke is batting away bugs. Stacey is practicing some dance move she probably just learned. Jenna is talking constantly even though no one seems to be listening.

"Miss Woo even let me borrow her Greek music CD!" I hear Jenna say as they get closer.

Stacey does a graceful spin and lands next to me on the bench. Jenna plops down beside her and pulls a clipboard out of her backpack. "My parents are going to *love* this," she says, scribbling notes on the clipboard.

"Love what?" I ask.

"The dance we're going to do for Greek Day," Jenna says.

"Oh, I know!" Jolene chimes in, sitting down on the grass. "Let's make up a dance about that goofy boy who built wings with *wax* and then tried to fly to the sun." She laughs. "Typical."

Meeka laughs, too, and sits down next to Jolene. "Or the one about the wicked goddess who left a golden apple at a party and—"

"I'm gonna be a cyclops," Randi cuts in. "With Rusty. We're gonna glue a googly eye on our forehead and tell jokes."

"Fine," Jenna says, looking up from her clipboard, "but you're going to be in my dance, too. All the do-good nymphs are." She glances at Meeka and Jolene. "And I've already decided which myth we'll do."

"Which one?" Stacey asks.

"We're going to dance the myth about Gaia, goddess of the Earth, and how she saved her grandson, Zeus, from being eaten by his father," Jenna replies. "I've still got my Gaia costume from Brooke's party, so I'll be her." She makes another note on her clipboard.

"His father wanted to *eat* him?" Brooke says. She wrinkles her nose like a bug flew up it.

Jenna gives Brooke a look. "Don't you *ever* pay attention in class? Old lady Eddy told us that myth when she subbed for Mr. Crow. First, Zeus's dad ate his five oldest children, then he got tricked into eating a goat and a stone. He would have eaten Zeus, too, only I came along and saved the day."

Brooke shrugs. "Sounds like a fantasy."

I snort. "Sounds like a stomachache."

Randi looks up from dribbling ants. "I'll be Zeus!" she shouts.

Jenna shakes her head. "In this myth Zeus is only a baby. I need someone smaller." Jenna thinks for a moment. "Tom Sanders is the smallest kid in our class. Plus, he knows how to dance. I'll tell him to be Zeus." Jenna makes another note on her clipboard.

"Then I'll be his father!" Randi says. She picks up her basketball, brushes off the squished ants, and stuffs it under her shirt. She groans like she just ate five children, a goat, and a rock. "See?" she says, poking her belly. "I got *my* costume, too!"

Everyone laughs. Except Jenna. "Fine," she says. "You can be the father. Wear a toga over your basketball."

"What's a toga?" Brooke asks.

"It's Greek for bedsheet," I reply.

"What about me?" Stacey asks.

Jenna turns to Stacey. "You'll be a nymph." Then she looks at Brooke, Meeka, and Jolene. "So will you. After I hide baby Zeus in a cave, you have to take care of him."

"But I'm allergic to mold," Brooke says, swatting at a fly. "And caves are famous for it." She gives Jenna a sideways sneer. "Or don't you *ever* pay attention in science?"

Jenna rolls her eyes. "Not a *real* cave, Brooke. "We're going to use—"

"What about Ida?" Randi cuts in, drumming her basketball belly. "She still needs a part."

Jenna grins. "That's what I'm getting at. I have the *perfect* part for Ida."

I gulp.

"What?" the others ask, even though I'm perfectly happy not knowing what Jenna has in mind.

"Ida will be the *place* where I hide Zeus!" Jenna replies.

I give Jenna a very serious squint. "The *place*?"

Jenna nods. "I hide Zeus in a cave on *Mount Ida*. Isn't that perfect?"

"I can't be a *mountain*!" I say.

"Of course you can," Jenna says back. "All you have to do is stand still while we dance around you."

"Won't people wonder why she's just *standing* there?" Stacey asks.

"Of course not," Jenna replies. "It will be obvious she's part of the scenery when they see her costume."

"Um...excuse me," I say. "I'm all out of mountain costumes."

"No, you're not," Jenna says. "Just paint a mountain on a box. Put it on. You're Mount Ida."

"I have to wear...a *box*?"

"Yes," Jenna says. "Like you wore to Brooke's party, remember? Only bigger, so Zeus can fit inside, too."

"Huh?"

Jenna taps her pen impatiently on her clipboard. "I hide Zeus in a *cave* on Mount Ida," she explains. "That's why Zeus has to be someone small, like Tom. He has to fit inside the box with you."

I jump up and punch my fists into my hips. "I am *not* wearing a box with a boy!" I shout.

I hear a gasp from the other girls.

Jenna's jaw tightens and her eyes narrow like fishhooks. "Fine," she says. "I'll make Rachel be Zeus. She's small and she's a girl."

"Rachel isn't in our class," I say. "And this is a clas—"

"My mother is still the PTA president, even though she's had to miss some meetings lately," Jenna interrupts. "If I say Rachel will be Zeus, then Rachel will be Zeus."

Jenna goes back to her clipboard.

I sink down on the bench and think about the box costume I wore to Brooke's party. I think about being mistaken for an end table and having punch cups piled on me. Then I think about wearing a box that's painted like a mountain. And standing there in front of my whole class. And all of our parents. And of Rachel squeezing inside it with me.

"But—," I start to say.

"Now that we've got *that* settled," Jenna continues, "it's time for our club meeting."

Jenna hooks her pen on her clipboard. "First, we need to award leaves for all our good deeds. Whoever gets the most leaves wins the special prize!"

Jenna sets down her clipboard and marches over to a bush. She starts yanking off leaves.

"What *is* the special prize?" Randi asks, scooting in next to Brooke on the bench. She rests an elbow on her basketball belly and starts picking at a scab. Each time she flicks a scab bit, Brooke flinches.

"You'll see," Jenna says, walking back to us with her handful of leaves. "I'll go first. 1. I picked up litter. 2. I got some kid her ball. 3. I helped old lady Eddy cross the street." Jenna pulls three leaves from her fist and sticks them in her green braids.

"Your turn, Stacey," Jenna says.

Stacey thinks for a minute. "Let's see... I helped Mr. Crow correct some papers," she says. "And I gave Ida my brownie at lunch." Stacey gives me a smile.

Jenna frowns and gives Stacey two leaves. "Put them in your hair, like me," she says.

Stacey sticks the leaves in her curls. Then she turns to me. "You're next, Ida."

"Um...," I say, trying to think of something good I did today. All I can think of is making the bus driver wait for Jenna and I don't think she'll be handing over any leaves for that.

"Hurry up," Jenna says. "We don't have all day."

I fidget, thinking. "Um...I watched gum."

"You *what*?" Jenna says.

I sit up a little. "I watched some girl's gum while she hung on the monkey bars. Saving her from a potential choking hazard."

"Wow," Jolene says. "I think saving someone from a potential choking hazard is worth *two* leaves!"

Meeka nods. "I think it's worth *three*!"

Brooke and Stacey nod, too. Randi gives me a drum roll on her belly.

Jenna just scowls and pulls one leaf from her fist. "One good deed, *one* leaf," she says. "That's the rule."

"Since when?" Brooke asks.

"Since now," Jenna says. "All in favor say, 'Aye.'"

No one says a word.

Jenna's jaw tightens. Everyone stays quiet.

Finally, Jenna pries two more leaves from her fist. She tosses all three leaves at me.

"Thanks," I say. I stick two of the leaves in my barrettes. I give the third one to Stacey.

Stacey smiles.

Brooke gasps. "Ida shared a leaf! That's another good deed!"

"Yeah!" Randi says. "Give her another leaf!"

Jenna clenches her fists so tight her knuckles whiten up like marbles in a sweat sock. "No!" she shouts.

"Why not?" Stacey asks, sticking the leaf I gave her into her hair.

"Because this is *my* club and I make the rules!" Jenna yanks the leaf back out of Stacey's hair and jabs it into mine.

Then she drops like a rock onto the grass. "Take your turn, Brooke," she says.

But even Brooke isn't much interested in earning leaves anymore. She, Meeka, Jolene, and Randi can only come up with three good deeds among them.

"I say Ida should get the special prize," Randi offers. She sticks her leaf to her scabby elbow.

Everyone turns to Jenna, waiting for her answer. Jenna frowns, but she opens her backpack. She pulls out half a bag of cookies. Vanilla.

"Here," she says, tossing the cookies onto my lap.

"*That's* the special prize?" Randi says. "They don't even have sprinkles!"

Jenna's face is so burning hot now that it boils up some tears. "Maybe my mother is too busy to bake, and my father doesn't have much experience shopping for cookies!" she yells. Then she grabs her backpack and marches away.

We all just sit there for a minute, watching her go.

"She forgot her clipboard," Stacey says quietly.

I open the cookie bag and pass the crumbs around.

Chapter 12

"I'm going to walk to Stacey's house after school so we can get her stuff for the weekend," I tell Mom the next morning. "And then we'll walk here."

"If you want, I can drive you there before my four o'clock piano lesson," Mom offers.

"Um...no thanks," I say. "We need to... um...get some exercise."

Mom grins. "Sounds good," she says.

I pick up my backpack and Jenna's clipboard and hurry out the door.

A few minutes later, Jenna marches up to the bus stop like usual.

"Here," I say, holding out her clipboard. "You forgot this yesterday."

She takes the clipboard from me. "I don't even

need it anymore," she says. "I've got the whole dance memorized."

"What dance?" Quinn asks.

"For the parents show on Greek Day," Jenna says. "My club is doing it."

"What club?" Tess asks.

"The Do-Good Nymphs," Jenna replies, shaking back her green braids. She's wearing her nymph fish shirt again. "Everyone's in it. Even Ida."

"Even me!" Rachel adds.

"You're only in the dance, Rachel," Jenna says. "*Not* my club."

Rachel ducks her head.

I give her shoulder a nudge. "Lucky you," I whisper.

"Me, Rusty, and Zane are doing the Trojan War for the program," Quinn says.

"How can you do a whole war?" I ask.

"We're just doing the part where the Trojans get tricked into thinking a giant wooden horse is a present from the enemy army. But really, the army is hiding inside it. We're gonna make a horse-shaped piñata, fill it up with plastic army guys, and bust it open!" Quinn takes a hard swing with an invisible bat.

Jenna huffs. "The Trojan War is a *legend,* not a myth."

Quinn shrugs. "Same diff. We still get to bust open a horse!"

The bus comes around the corner and Jenna steps up to the curb. Rachel tugs on my sleeve and hands me a sticky note with lots of scribbles on it. "There's no reason to worry," she says. "Everything will be fine."

Jenna rounds up all the nymphs before school to show us the dance she has memorized. Then, at recess, she shoos some second graders out of the pigpen so we can practice. "Randi, you stand over there and pretend to eat your children. Stacey, Meeka, Jolene, and Brooke, do the dance I showed you this morning. Ida, you stand in the middle and try not to get in the way."

Jenna makes us practice until the bell rings, which means I don't get any time with Stacey to talk about calling her dad tonight to tell him she's sick. At lunch, Jenna makes us eat quick and then patrol the lunchroom for food fights. During afternoon recess, we're back in the pigpen, practicing.

Later, Mr. Crow hands out shoe boxes and craft stuff so we can make pretend shrines. Mr. Crow told us *shrine* comes from a Latin word that means *box*. It's a place where gods and goddesses get worshipped by their fans. My shrine is for the god Ares because Mr. Crow also told us the Roman name for Ares is Mars and I figure any guy who gets a planet named after him deserves to get worshipped.

I'm busy gluing a cotton ball couch inside my shoe box so Ares will be comfortable when a note lands on my desk.

> Did you remember to plug in the mermaid last night?
>
> S.

I glance across the aisle at Stacey and her shrine for Athena, the goddess of wisdom. She gives me a sideways smile. I write my reply and toss it back.

> Yep. Extra early. My dad hadn't even fallen asleep in front of the TV yet.
>
> I.

I squeeze a square of glue onto my shoe box floor and sprinkle glitter over it for a rug. Another note appears.

> Meet me at the pigpen after school. Only don't let Jenna see you. She wanted me to come to her house this weekend to work on props for the dance, so I had to tell her I'm going to my dad's right after school and won't be back until late on Sunday.
>
> S.
>
> P.S. We are going to have so much fun!

As soon as I finish drawing Ares on a craft stick and propping him up on the couch, Mr. Crow tells us it's time to line up for music. "Why didn't you tell Jenna you're staying with me?" I whisper to Stacey as we get in line.

"Because she might mention it to her mom, and then it might get back to Kelli, and that might cause problems," Stacey whispers back.

"I thought the mermaid would make sure we don't have any problems," I say.

Before Stacey can answer, Jenna steps up to us. "Passing notes during class is against the rules," she says. "So is talking in line."

She hands a note to each of us.

Do-Good Nymphs Dance Practice
When: Monday, after school
Where: Jenna's House
Who: All Do-Good Nymphs
(Attendance is required!!!)

"Be sure to tell your parents you have to be there," Jenna tells us as we walk down the hall. "Oh, and Ida, you should come over to my house tomorrow so we can paint your box."

I gulp. "Um...I can't," I say. "I'm going to... be busy." I glance at Stacey.

"Doing what?" Jenna asks.

"Um...helping my mom. With some hammering."

Jenna frowns. "Can't your dad help her with that?"

"Um...no," I reply. "He's not allowed to hammer. It's a rule."

111

Jenna lifts her chin and I see it quiver a little. "Never mind," she says, pushing past us.

Stacey gives my arm a squeeze. "That was quick thinking, Ida!" she says. "Good thing the mermaid's helping us, huh?"

"Good thing," I reply.

When we get to Stacey's house after school, her Grandma Tootie is snoozing in front of the TV. We sneak into Stacey's bedroom and she calls her dad to tell him she's sick and needs to stay home. Then she calls Kelli and tells her she talked to her dad and he's going out of town, unexpectedly. Then she asks if she can spend the weekend with me instead. Five minutes later, we have all of Stacey's stuff packed up and we are heading for the door.

"Is that you, Stacey?" Grandma Tootie looks up from her recliner.

We stop and turn around. "Yep," Stacey says. "Dad called to tell me something came up this weekend, so Kelli said I can stay at Ida's instead."

"Your dad called? When?"

"Just a few minutes ago," Stacey replies.

"Huh," Grandma Tootie says. "I didn't hear the phone."

"Well, you were sleeping," Stacey says. "So I picked it up fast."

Stacey gives her grandma a smile.

I give my shoes the once-over.

Grandma Tootie picks up the remote and changes the channel on the TV. "Well, you girls have fun," she says.

"We will!" Stacey says back and yanks me out the door.

When we get to my house, my mom is teaching piano and my dad is still at work, so we grab a snack from the kitchen, dump Stacey's stuff in my bedroom, and head to the attic. That's because on the way here Stacey had the best idea ever.

We push boxes to one end of the attic to make a secret room. I unroll an old rug, and Stacey sets the wobbly piano bench on it. "This bench can be the shrine," she says. "We have to make it really nice so the mermaid will want to stay here *permanently*."

We hurry downstairs to the kitchen for tape and aluminum foil. Then we go back and cover the bench with it. I find an old string of Christmas tree lights and hang it on the wall behind the bench/shrine. We find some fake spiders and doll body parts and scatter them around because that's the kind of stuff evil mermaids like. Then we run to my room, partly because all those spiders and body parts creep us out and partly to get the mermaid. We set her on the shiny bench/shrine and plug her in. The whole place glows with her evilness so we know she likes it here.

"We should write her some fan mail," I say.

"Oooo...good idea," Stacey says back. She dashes over to my dad's tool bench and grabs a jar of pens and pencils. "I'll get some paper from your room!" she says, heading for the door.

"Wait!" I say. "I have a better idea."

I take the jar and dump out the pens and pencils. "Fill this up with water in the bathroom," I say, handing her the empty jar. "And grab a roll of toilet paper. I'll get some markers."

Stacey gives me a puzzled look.

"Mermaids live in water, right?" I say.

Stacey nods.

"So, if you want to send a mermaid fan mail, the best way is with water."

Stacey still looks confused, but she flies out the door with the jar.

I run to my room and dig through my desk. I

find two purple markers that smell like sour grape gummy worms.

I head for the door. I stop and give George a smile.

George does not give me one back.

"Don't be jealous, George," I say. "Someday I'll build you a shrine, too."

George doesn't budge.

I take off for the attic, sniffing my markers the whole way.

Stacey sets the jar of water next to the mermaid and I hand her a marker. We tear off some toilet paper and get busy writing.

Dear Mermaid,
  We built this shrine just for you.
  It took almost 1 hour or 2.
  Do you like it? We do!
                              — Stacey

Dear Mermaid,
  We are your biggest fans. Let us know if you need a new light bulb or anything.
                              Ida

We crumple up our notes and drop them into the jar. Right away the water turns a very magical purple.

Stacey gasps. "The mermaid did that!"

I nod.

A minute later, our writing fades away and all that's left is the paper, floating like clouds in a magical purple sky.

Chapter 13

When I wake up the next morning, I look over the edge of my bed. Stacey is still asleep in a sleeping bag on the floor. I lay back and think about all the fun we had last night. Building the shrine. Guarding the mermaid from wicked screwdrivers. Making her offerings of root beer and candy bars.

I push off my covers and tiptoe to my desk. I pick up a pencil and open my sketchbook. I flip past the drawings I did at the park and write *The Secret Mermaid Club* across the top of a new page. Then I draw two girls. I give one straight hair and one curly hair, but I give them both the same smile. Then I get out my colored pencils and start filling them in.

"What are you doing?"

I turn to see Stacey sitting up and rubbing her eyes.

"I'm making a sign for the shrine," I say, coloring Stacey's eyes brown and mine blue. I hold it up to show her.

"Nice," Stacey says. "But aren't you forgetting someone?"

"Who?" I ask, studying the picture.

"The mermaid!" Stacey says, stretching.

"Oh, yeah," I say, turning back to my desk. Then I draw the mermaid, a little smaller and off to one side.

"I'm starving," Stacey says, crawling out from her sleeping bag.

"Me, too. Let's get some breakfast and then go back to the attic and start having more fun!"

Stacey crawls over the blankets that fell off my bed and heads out the door. I close my sketchbook and wade after her. I stop when I step on something squishy.

I look down and see George under my foot. I pick him up and unsquish his stomach. "Be careful, George," I say. "Or you'll get hurt."

I fluff up the blankets and set George on top, like he's king of the mountain.

My foot snags a corner of the mountain on the way out and George tumbles back to where he started.

Dad makes pancakes for breakfast with whipped-cream hair, strawberry eyes, and chocolate chip mouths.

"I'm going to bake cookies this morning," Mom says as we carry our plates to the sink. "Want to help?"

"No, thanks," I say. "We've got some important stuff to do . . . um . . . upstairs."

Me and Stacey take off for my bedroom, throw on some clothes, and head to the attic.

"Let's pretend the shrine is hidden in a deep, dark cave," Stacey says, finding a flashlight on the workbench. "And we're searching for it."

"Okay," I say. "We can draw a secret map on one of the boxes, and use it to find her!"

I grab the pens and pencils we dumped out of the jar last night and we start drawing.

Before long, we're crawling so deep into the cave we hardly even hear the doorbell when it rings. And a few minutes later, when my mom calls our names from downstairs, it's like she's a million miles away.

"Let's pretend we didn't hear her," Stacey says.

"The cookies are probably done," I say back. "If we don't go downstairs, she'll bring them up here. And then she'll see what we're doing and it won't be a secret anymore."

Stacey flicks off the flashlight. "You're right," she says. "Let's go and hurry back!"

We race each other downstairs. As soon as we hit the bottom step, our feet freeze.

My mom is standing just inside our front door. So is Kelli.

"Kelli?" Stacey says. "What are you doing here?"

"I was just going to ask *you* the same question," Kelli says. She folds her arms across her chest. "Guess who called me this morning?"

I hear Stacey swallow. "Who?" she asks.

"Your dad," Kelli says. "He wanted to know if you were still *sick*."

"Oh," Stacey says, quietly.

My skin starts to prickle and I could use a little air.

Kelli continues, "I told him, 'Stacey's not sick, and she told me you were going out of town.'"

Stacey stares at the step.

My mom looks at me. "Ida, did you know about this?"

I fidget. And nod.

Kelli starts pacing. She runs her fingers through her spiky hair. "What have I said about the *lying*, Stace?"

Stacey doesn't answer.

"Get in the car," Kelli snaps. "I'll get your stuff."

Stacey's eyes are bright with tears. She storms out the door.

My mom zeroes in on me as she follows Kelli upstairs.

If I was wax, I would be a puddle right now.

I wait until Mom walks Kelli out to her car. Then I run to the attic. I put away the flashlight and pick up the pens and pencils and candy wrappers that are still scattered across the floor. I walk over to the mermaid and put my hand on her glowing head. "Please don't let her be too mad," I say and pull out her plug.

I'm lying on my bed when Mom walks into my

room a few minutes later. She sits down next to me. "We need to talk," she says.

I sit up and fiddle with George's tail.

"Tell me what happened," Mom says. "*Everything.*"

So I tell her the whole story. Only I leave out the part about the mermaid. "Stacey's my best friend," I say. "I didn't want to let her down."

"Lying lets everyone down, Ida," Mom says. "Sometimes you have to stand up *to* a friend if you want to stand up *for* her."

"But I don't think Stacey even likes going to her dad's," I say. "It just reminds her that they're not a family anymore."

"Ida, they're still a family," Mom says. "They still need to work stuff out." She reaches over and brushes back my bangs. "I'll talk to Dad. Then we'll let this one go. But if you ever do something like this again—"

"I won't," I say. "I promise."

Chapter 14

On Monday morning, I walk past the broken water fountain. Stacey isn't there. I check the girls' bathroom, but she isn't there, either.

"Did you hear?" Tom says to me as I walk into our classroom. "Miss Woo invited our class to have our Greek Day at her studio next Sunday. Mr. Crow is running off notes about it right now!"

Tom pokes his thumb toward the board where Mr. Crow hangs up drawings and other stuff we make. Tom's school picture is attached to the body of a cartoon god, riding in a chariot. "I call him A*Tom*o," Tom says, smiling. "Cool, huh?"

"The coolest," I say, and smile back.

"It gives me an idea for Greek Day," Tom continues. "In fact, now that we'll be doing the program at Miss Woo's studio, I have a *big* idea!"

Before Tom can tell me what his big idea is, the bell rings and everyone heads to their desks. Everyone except Stacey. She's nowhere in sight.

But Jenna is. I can feel her eyes heating up the back of my head.

I turn to look at her. "What?" I ask.

"*Hammering* all weekend, huh?" she says. She shifts her eyes away, but my head still burns.

Mr. Crow walks in with a stack of notes. He's handing them out when Stacey hurries into the room. "Sorry I'm late," she says to Mr. Crow.

"You're right on time," he replies, handing her a note.

Mr. Crow starts explaining about having our parents program at Miss Woo's. I grab a scrap of paper out of my desk and write a note. I toss it onto Stacey's desk.

What happened when you got home on Saturday?

I.

I wait a minute and then read the note that sails back.

124

I got grounded! For the rest of the week. No phone calls, no going anywhere with friends. I can't even go to Jenna's house today to practice our dance. Kelli called Mrs. Drews to explain. So now I'm sure Jenna's not speaking to me.

S.

P.S. Did you get in trouble?

I write another note and pass it back.

I didn't get grounded, but if I ever do anything like that again I'll get buried.

I.

P.S. There are worse things than not having Jenna Drews speaking to you.

Stacey reads my note and glances at me. Then she glances over her shoulder at Jenna.

"Hi, Jenna," she whispers.

Jenna glances at Stacey's left ear. "No talking during class," she says. Then she glances at me. "No passing notes, either." Then she goes back to staring at the chalkboard.

I guess Jenna decides to give the do-good nymphs the day off, because she doesn't make us meet at the pigpen for recess. In fact, I don't even see her at recess. And at lunch, when we all sit together at our usual table, Jenna just chews her veggie burger without one word about the greasy meatballs the rest of us are eating. She doesn't even lift an eyebrow when Brooke and Stacey make friendship bracelets out of their spaghetti, or when Jolene and Meeka stick cucumber slices to their earlobes, or when Randi catapults cherry tomatoes at the boys with her spoon.

After school, Jenna announces, "See you on the bus," and then walks off without even lining up Randi, Brooke, Meeka, Jolene, and me for the trip to her house.

Stacey walks to the bus with me. "Can I call you tonight and tell you how practice went?" I ask.

Stacey shakes her head. "No phone calls, remember?"

"Can't we even go to the Purdee Good this week for a giant cookie?"

"I can't go anywhere except school and dance class on Thursday. Then on Friday my dad is picking me up right after school and taking me to his place for the weekend."

"He'll bring you back for the program on Sunday, right?" I ask.

"Unfortunately," Stacey mumbles.

"Don't you want him to come?"

Stacey sighs. "Yes, but he will want to bring Tanya. And then Kelli will see her and be even madder at me for not telling her about the girlfriend situation." Stacey sighs again. "It's all kind of…complicated."

I fidget a little, thinking about the talk me and my mom had on Saturday. "Maybe you should just tell your dad to talk to your mom? About Tanya?"

"So Kelli can be mad at him, too?" Stacey says. She shakes her head. "It's better if she doesn't know everything."

Stacey walks off and I climb onto the bus. I sink down next to Rachel.

"You look sweaty," Rachel says, studying me.

I blow my bangs. "Yeah, it's hot out there today."

———

A few minutes later we're all walking into Jenna's house. Biscuit, her hyper little dog, runs circles around us, jumping and barking. Must be a boy dog.

"That you, Jenna?" Mr. Drews calls from the living room.

"Who else?" Jenna grumbles back.

The other girls take turns holding Biscuit. I peek into the living room and see Mr. Drews sitting on the couch with his bare feet pointing toward the TV. He's wearing pajama pants and a WORK FOR PEACE T-shirt. But the only thing I see him working on is a bag of potato chips.

Rachel skips past me and climbs onto his lap.

"Hi, kiddo," he says, giving her cheek a rub with his scratchy chin.

Rachel munches on a chip. "Where's Mom?" she asks.

"Bringing home the bacon," Mr. Drews replies. He punches up the volume on the remote and grabs another chip out of the bag.

"Everyone's here to practice our dance," Jenna barks from behind me.

"Mmm-hmm," Mr. Drews says. "Mom left a note."

Jenna crosses her arms and taps her toe. "Well? Is there anything to eat?"

"Cookies in the kitchen," Mr. Drews replies, giving the remote another punch. Rachel settles back against his shoulder. Biscuit scampers in and begs for chips. Jenna whips around and walks away.

We follow Jenna into the kitchen. Plastic grocery bags slump near the back door. Cracker boxes, gummy snacks, and soup cans peek out of their tops. Crusty pots and milky cereal bowls are stacked in the sink. Sticky notes cover the refrigerator door with messages like BUY DOG FOOD, TAKE JENNA TO SCOUTS, and DO LAUNDRY! written on them. A bag of vanilla cookies spills across the counter. Another sticky note is next to it.

Jenna,
I'll be home late again. Make sure Rachel eats something GREEN with supper.
Help her get ready for bed, okay?
Love,
Mom

Jenna studies the note like it's a science experiment. Then she marches to the kitchen doorway. "If you're not going to *bake* cookies, could you at least *buy* some that don't taste like tree bark?!" she shouts.

"What?!" Mr. Drews shouts back.

"Never mind!" Jenna snaps and marches back to us.

"What's up with your dad?" Brooke asks. "Doesn't he have to work?"

"He's taking some time off," Jenna grumbles.

"Man, that would be great," Randi says, nibbling a cookie. "My dad and me could play basketball 24/7 if he took some time off."

"It's *not* great," Jenna says. "Not when your dad is supposed to do the stuff your mom usually does, only he does it all wrong." She grabs the bag of cookies. "C'mon. We've got work to do."

Jenna marches out the door into the backyard.

We shoot glances at each other and follow along.

Jenna tosses the cookie bag onto a picnic table and starts picking up scattered toys. She chucks them into a vegetable garden that takes up one corner of the yard. A tire swing hangs from a tree in another corner. Jolene and Randi spin Meeka on it until she squeals. Brooke throws herself into a lounge chair that's under the tree. She picks up a Frisbee Jenna missed and starts fanning her face. I shuffle around in the weedy grass. It could use a crew cut.

"Ida, you stand there," Jenna says, pointing to a cleared off spot just past the picnic table. "We need to practice the part where I dance on stage with Zeus and the nymphs dance around me." She looks at Brooke, Meeka, and Jolene. "Just be sure to leave room for Stacey," she adds. Then she turns toward the house. "Rachel!" she hollers. "Get out here!"

"I want to be a goddess," Brooke complains from behind her fan. "Aphrodite or Athena. Not some no-name nymph."

"There's only *one* goddess in this myth," Jenna says. "Gaia. Zeus's grandmother. Me."

"Brooke could be Zeus's mom," Randi says, giving Meeka another spin. "She must have been a goddess."

"Yeah," Brooke says. "Where's his mom?"

"She probably went shopping for bacon," Rachel says, coming out the back door. She's wearing a sparkly blue dance costume with a puffy tutu. She's carrying three Kens, two Barbies, and one stuffed poodle.

Jenna studies her sister and sighs. "Rachel, why are you wearing your old recital costume?" she asks.

"Because you said I got to be in your dance," Rachel replies. "And you said I got to be a boy, so there you go. Blue is for boys." She lines up her toys on the picnic table.

Jenna gives her sister a huff. Then she turns back to Brooke. "You can be the *head* nymph," she says. "You can even wear one of your pageant crowns."

Brooke thinks this idea over for about one second and says, "Okay!"

Then Jenna turns to me. "Try your box on, Ida," she says, pointing to a large brown box that's sitting next to the picnic table. "You'll have to pretend it looks like a mountain since you were too busy to help me paint it."

I walk over to the box and look inside. A hundred scribbled sticky notes are stuck to it.

I glance at Rachel. She glances back at me. "It's a good box," she says, smiling. Then she puts a sticky note on the poodle.

I'm about to tell Jenna I can't wear a box with no holes to see through when something catches my eye.

A bush on the other side of the yard is looking at me. Two sparkly eyes blink through its branches. A moment later, Stacey peeks around the side of the bush and gives me a secret smile. Then she disappears around the house.

I look back at the other girls. Brooke, Meeka, and Jolene are too busy learning a new step Jenna just invented to notice Stacey. And Randi is too busy feeding cookies to the squirrels. And Rachel is too busy telling Ken to give Barbie a hand with the laundry.

"Um...," I say, loudly. "I need to...go to... the bathroom."

Jenna gives me a glance. "Hurry up," she says. "We'll need you in a minute."

I nod and walk quickly to the back door. I go inside the house, but I don't go to the bathroom. I tiptoe to the living room and peek inside. Mr. Drews is still watching TV. Biscuit looks up from his lap and whines at me. Mr. Drews feeds him another chip. I sneak past and open the front door. Then I close it behind me, carefully, like it's made of glass.

I stand on the porch and look around for Stacey.

Snap!

I turn toward the sound and see Stacey crouching behind a big tree with a broken stick in her hand. She waves.

I glance around, run across the yard, and dive behind the tree.

"What are you doing here?" I ask.

"Grandma Tootie fell asleep in her recliner," Stacey says, all breathless. "The mermaid gave me the idea to play outside, so I wouldn't disturb her."

"That was thoughtful of her," I reply.

Stacey nods. "So I went outside. And *then* the mermaid gave me the idea to go for a little walk. So I did. And, just like that, she led me right here!"

"Wow," I say. "Only you're grounded so you should probably go back home, right? Before your grandma wakes up?"

"Probably," Stacey says. "Only I thought it would

be fun to do something together *first.* Just the two of us!" Stacey's eyes go all wide and hopeful.

"But—," I start to say.

"Let's go to your house!" Stacey jumps up. "And play in your attic!"

"My mom's teaching piano lessons today," I say. "And it would be a major *catastrophe* if she caught us sneaking around. Trust me."

"If we go in through the back door she won't see us," Stacey says.

I fidget a little. "I promised I wouldn't sneak around anymore and if we get caught—"

"We won't get caught," Stacey says. "Remember? The mermaid?"

"Oh, yeah," I mumble and fidget some more. "I forgot."

"Just for a little while. *Please?* I'm going crazy stuck at home."

I sigh. And nod.

Stacey gives my arm a friendly squeeze. "Quick! Follow me!"

Stacey sneak-runs to another tree, then to a birdbath, and then to a parked car. She crouches behind the car and waves me in.

I get ready to follow her, but before I take off I glance back at Jenna's house.

Jenna is standing on her front porch, looking right at me.

I gulp and glance at Stacey. Her feet disappear around the side of the car.

I look back at Jenna and wait for her to start yelling. I think about Mr. Drews coming out onto the porch to see what all the yelling is about. And Jenna telling him. And making him call my mom because I'm breaking about a million rules. And the look on my mom's face when she comes to get me and take me home.

But Jenna doesn't yell. She just walks back inside the house and closes the door, carefully, like it's made of glass.

Chapter
15

Stacey's right. My mom is so busy teaching piano she doesn't notice us sneaking into the house and up to the attic.

"We better be quiet," I whisper to Stacey as we tiptoe across the floor. "If my mom hears us creaking around she'll come up here for sure."

Stacey nods and sits down on the floor. I sit down, too, and glance at the mermaid. I realize it's been days since I plugged her in.

After a few minutes of sitting, my butt realizes how hard the floor is. It shoots a few complaints to my legs.

Then my head realizes how hot it is up here.

And how boring it is to be so quiet.

And how thirsty it makes me.

And how hungry.

And how I really do need to go to the bathroom.

After the piano music finally stops and I hear my mom opening and closing drawers in the bedroom below us, I turn to Stacey. She's peeling aluminum foil off the shrine and flicking the bits around.

"This is fun and all," I whisper. "But maybe you should get back home before your grandma figures out you're gone?"

Stacey sighs and flicks another bit. "I suppose," she says. "But let's do this again tomorrow, okay?"

"Um...I don't know," I say. "I mean, I might be busy."

"Doing what?" Stacey asks.

I think for a minute. "Well, tomorrow's Tuesday, which means we'll probably have tacos for supper. So there will be a lot of tomato chopping that needs to get done."

"Maybe on Wednesday, then?" Stacey asks.

"Maybe," I say. "But my mom doesn't give piano lessons on Wednesdays so, honestly, she could be anywhere in the house."

Just then, the phone rings. I hear my mom pick it up.

"Hello?" she says. "Tootie! Hi!"

I glance at Stacey. "Your grandma?"

Stacey nods and we press our ears to the floor so we can hear what my mom is saying.

"No, Stacey's not here. Ida's at Jenna's house, practicing their Greek dance. Uh-huh... Uh-huh... I see. Well, maybe Stacey went to Jenna's house anyway? Why don't you call over there and check. And if she shows up here, I'll send her straight home."

Stacey looks at me. "Time to go," she whispers.

"*Fast,*" I whisper back.

As soon as we hear my mom clattering in the kitchen, we sneak downstairs and out the front door. Stacey takes off and I wait on the porch for a minute. Then I stomp back inside. "Hi, Mom!" I shout, slamming the door. "I'm home! From Jenna's house! Where I've been all afternoon!"

Then I run upstairs to the bathroom, fast, so I can avoid any questions or accidents.

I'm working on my second helping of macaroni and cheese at supper when the doorbell rings. I hurry to answer it in case Stacey decided to come sneaking around again.

It's not Stacey.

It's Jenna Drews.

Jenna holds my backpack out to me. "You forgot this," she says.

"Um...oops," I say. I take the backpack from her. "Thanks."

Jenna just lifts her chin. Then she glances off to the side. "The paint's still wet," she says.

I step onto the porch and see a box sitting next to her. It's the same box that was sitting by her picnic table earlier, only now it's painted on all four sides. No matter which way you look at it, you see Mount Ida.

"Wow," I say, walking around the box. "How did you get it painted so fast?"

Jenna shrugs. "Rachel helped a little." Then she points to a hole that's cut out of the top. "That's your head hole. If you wear a white hoodie and tuck your chin, you'll look snowcapped."

"Good idea," I say, and give her half a smile.

Jenna glances away. "Rachel thought of it."

She turns to leave. Then she stops and turns halfway back. "I told the other girls you were sick," she says. "So you had to leave early."

"Oh," I say, shifting my backpack. "Um... thanks."

Jenna gives me a quick nod. "But that's the last time I lie for you."

She turns away and marches down the steps.

Later, I don't sleep the greatest. A green cyclops keeps eyeing me. I try to hide from it, but everything I duck behind fades away.

When it's finally morning, I can hardly get out of bed, partly because I'm still tired and partly because my sheets are twisted around me like a toga.

I bump into Mount Ida on the way to my dresser. I hauled the box up here last night even though some of the wet paint rubbed off onto my favorite shirt.

I study the box for a minute. I feel bad about not helping to paint it. And about sneaking away from Jenna's.

I glance up at George. He's sitting on top of the box like a mountain climber.

"She cut me a head hole," I say to him. "Even after I snuck out."

George watches me from the peak.

I trudge to my dresser and open a drawer. I dig around for my second favorite shirt. When I pull it out, my No-Good Nymphs shirt comes along for the ride. I hold it up and study the nymph—spiders, fangs, and all.

I glance at George again.

He looks past me to my desk.

I walk over to it. I pull a black marker out of a drawer and lay the shirt on the floor.

I scribble over the spiders. And make their legs longer and wavy so they look like highlights in the nymph's hair.

I change her capital *V* eyebrow into bangs.

And put braces on her fangs.

Then I change the *N* in No-Good back into a *D*. I frown a little because it looks more like an *O* that swallowed a *Z* sideways. But sometimes sideways is the best you can do.

I pick up the shirt and show it to George. "Better?" I ask.

George studies the shirt.

"Better," I say.

Then I fold it up and put it back in my drawer.

Even though Stacey believes me when I tell her I'm too busy to sneak around with her after school, I keep myself extra busy all day Tuesday, so there won't be time for the subject to come up again. I clean the hamster cage before class. I volunteer to make crepe-paper banners for Greek Day during morning recess. I eat lunch fast and then patrol the cafeteria, looking for second graders who need a hand opening their milk cartons. For afternoon recess, I clean the hamster cage again.

If Jenna is making the Do-Good Nymphs practice the Greek dance and do good deeds, I'm too busy to notice. Which works out good because, like usual, I'm avoiding Jenna, too. Only today it feels different. Like I'm not avoiding her because *she's* been a jerk. But because *I* have.

Wednesday is basically a repeat of Tuesday. Hamster cage. Milk cartons. Crepe-paper banners. Cyclops dreams. But on Thursday when Mr. Crow is setting up a video called *All About Greece,* a note sails onto my desk.

We haven't hardly talked since Monday! I'm so tired of being grounded. At least I get to go to ballet class today. And then we get to practice for our Greek Day dance afterward! Maybe we should ask the mermaid to make something extra fun happen, just for us, tomorrow?

S.

I pretend to be very busy looking for a pencil until the video starts. Then I pretend to be very interested in learning all about Greece. Afterward, when Mr. Crow asks for a volunteer to bring the video back to the library, my hand shoots up. It shoots up again when he asks for volunteers to paint the cardboard pillars he built for Greek Day. Quinn, Meeka, and Joey are done with their pillars by the end of our first recess. I do mine extra slow so I have to work on it during our second recess, too.

Chapter

16

After school, I stick close to Randi as we walk with the other girls to Miss Woo's so we can practice our Greek dance as soon as their class is done. Jenna and Stacey are in the lead. Brooke, Meeka, and Jolene come next. Me, Randi, and her basketball bring up the rear. She spins the ball on her finger as we walk along.

"I could never learn how to do that," I say, watching the ball spin.

"It's not so hard," Randi says, catching the ball. "If Brooke can learn, anyone can."

Brooke looks over her shoulder and gives Randi a squint. "Ha, ha," she says.

Randi grins.

"When did you teach Brooke how to spin a basketball?" I ask.

"Last weekend," Randi says. "When she slept over."

I pull Randi to a stop. "*Brooke* spent the night at *your* house? On purpose?"

"Sure," she says. "Lots of times. When my mom and dad work the weekend night shift Jade stays over with me and my brothers. Brooke usually comes, too."

"But why would Brooke do that?" I ask. "I mean...it seems like you're not the best of friends."

Randi shrugs. "So?" She spins the ball on her finger again. "There's no rule that says you gotta be best friends to sleep over."

Randi glances down the sidewalk at the other girls. Jenna and Stacey walk into Miss Woo's. Brooke, Meeka, and Jolene are nearly there. "Hey, Brooke!" Randi hollers. "Show Ida your spin!"

Brooke stops and turns around. Randi bounces the ball to her. Brooke catches it and gives it a spin on one of her polished fingers. A few seconds later it wobbles off and bounces back down the sidewalk.

"Needs work," Randi says, scooping up the

ball. Brooke does a pageant bow anyway and heads inside.

"Hey, look!" Randi says when we catch up to the others. "Mount Ida! Doing a flip!" She points to my costume that's sitting upside down by a bench in the entryway.

I nod. "My mom said she'd drop it off for me." A cardboard lightning bolt is sticking out of the box and I see Jenna's green leotard, vines, and a rock sitting on the bench. "Somebody must have dropped off Jenna's stuff, too," I add, but Randi has already wandered into the studio.

"Sweet!" she shouts, bouncing her basketball on the big wooden floor like she's in a gym. The other girls drop their stuff by the bench and head to the far end of the studio where Miss Woo is talking to Tom and some other dancers.

I sit down on the bench and watch Randi dribble her ball and fake-shoot at an invisible basket. Pretty soon, Miss Woo has all the dancers stand along a wooden bar, facing a wall of mirrors. I can see both sides of them as they lift their arms and bend their knees. Stacey's back looks long and loose, like wet paint on dry paper. Jenna's back looks stiff and straight, like she could bend that bar if she wanted to.

Thump! Thumpthumpthump...

I glance toward my box and see the lightning bolt jiggle.

I walk over to the box and peek inside.

"Hi, Ida!" Rachel smiles up at me.

"Hi, Rachel," I say back. "What are you doing in there?"

"Playing." Rachel holds up her poodle. Three Kens and two Barbies are riding on its back. "My dad dropped me off on his way to the bait shop," she says. "We needed eggs."

I give her a smile. "Do you want to sit on the bench with me?"

"No, thanks," Rachel says. "I like it in here. It's cozy."

"Hey, Ida! Think fast!"

I look up and see a basketball bulleting straight at my nose. I lift my hands and the ball bounces off my arm. It rolls across the studio floor.

"Oops," Randi says. "I guess you weren't ready."

"I probably wouldn't have caught it even if I was," I say and take off after the ball.

All the dancers have moved to the center of the studio. The ball zigzags between their legs and so do I. It finally comes to a stop at the tiny feet of Miss Woo.

"Did you lose something?" she asks.

I scoop up the ball. "Sorry," I say. "It got away from us." I glance back at Randi. She's swinging the lightning bolt around like a sword.

Miss Woo glances at Randi, too. "Would you and your friend like to join the class?" she asks.

"Um...no, thanks," I reply. "I've never been very good with tights. And Randi was born to play basketball. Or run a restaurant."

Miss Woo gives me the hint of a smile. "I meant, would you like to join us just for *today*?" She takes the basketball from me and motions to Randi. Randi drops the lightning bolt and gallops over.

Miss Woo stands us side by side in the last row. Actually, we *are* the last row. "Just do what they do," she says, pointing to the others, and walks away.

A moment later, music starts playing and everyone starts moving. Back and forth. Up and down. They look like paper dolls cut from the same strip of paper.

I start moving, too. So does Randi. Back and up. Forth and down. We are cut from different paper. Trust me.

"Meeka, extend your legs!" Miss Woo calls out. "Brooke, point your toes! Jenna, pull in your bum!"

Bum is the ballet word for butt.

"Hey, Ida," Randi says. "How's this?" She extends her leg and points her high-top. Then she kicks Jenna right in the bum. Jenna whips around and I see fireworks.

"Watch it!" she snaps at Randi.

"I was," Randi says, grinning. "And then I kicked it."

Tom Sanders is dancing in front of me, so I try to copy him, even though he is a boy. Before long, I'm only one knee bend and two pointed toes behind. Tom looks over his shoulder at me. "Fun, huh?" he says.

I smile a little and nod because, actually, it's not so bad.

After class, Tom and some of the other dancers get their stuff and go. Rachel crawls out of the box and picks up her lightning bolt. Stacey, Brooke, Meeka, and Jolene are already wearing their nymph costumes—white leotards, white tights, and one rhinestone tiara.

I pull up my white hoodie and put on my box. Randi pulls a bedsheet out of her backpack. It's covered with spaceships and green aliens. She wraps it on. Jenna rolls her eyes.

"Here, Ida," Jenna says, handing me a piece of paper. "Memorize this while I put on my costume."

"Huh?" I say, looking at all the writing on the paper.

"You're the first one on stage, so it makes sense for you to introduce our dance to the audience."

"But mountains can't talk so wouldn't it make more sense if—"

"I'll decide what mountains can and can't do," Jenna says, walking off.

Just then, Miss Woo walks up to us with a clipboard. "I need to know how many guests will be here for the program," she says. "I want to be sure I have enough chairs set up and crowns made."

"Crowns?" Brooke says.

"I told Mr. Crow I would make traditional Greek olive branch crowns for all the guests," Miss Woo explains.

"I'm allergic to olives," Brooke says.

151

Miss Woo smiles. "They won't be real olive branches," she says.

"In that case, sign my family up for three," Brooke says. "Mom, Dad, and Jade. I already have a crown." She adjusts her tiara.

We all start giving Miss Woo numbers and she writes them on her clipboard.

"Just my mom and grandma," Stacey says when it's her turn.

"Not your father?" Miss Woo replies.

"No...um...he's busy that night. Actually, he's on a trip. With my brother. They won't be back in time for the program."

Miss Woo nods and makes another mark on her clipboard. "I'll get the rest of the numbers from Mr. Crow," she says.

Jenna reappears wearing her vines. Miss Woo turns to her. "Shall I start your music?" Jenna gives her a nod and Miss Woo walks away.

I walk over to Stacey. "I thought you had to go to your dad's this weekend," I whisper.

"I do," she whispers back.

"How can you, if he's on a trip?"

"He's not. I just said that because I know he won't be here."

"Why not?"

"Because I told him the program got canceled."

"*What?*"

Stacey pulls me away from the other girls. "I told my dad that Mr. Crow has been sick lately, so he canceled the program. Now I don't have to worry about inviting Tanya. All I have to do is make sure he drives me to Kelli's early on Sunday. Then I'll have time to hide Kelli's camera so she can't send pictures of the program to my dad. That way, he'll never know there really *was* a program and—"

"Stacey—stop!" I suddenly say. "You can't hide the program from your dad and take your mom's camera and—"

"Relax, Ida," Stacey says. "The mermaid will take care of—"

Before Stacey can say another word, I grab the bottom of my box and throw it off. It tumbles across the floor.

"Whoa!" Randi shouts, jumping back, "Volcanic!"

The other girls jump back, too.

I plant my feet and zero in on Stacey. "You can't keep saying the mermaid makes stuff happen!"

I shout. "It's only true because we decided it's true! *We* make stuff happen by lying and sneaking around!"

Greek music starts playing through the speakers, but nobody starts dancing. We're all too busy watching Stacey grab her stuff and run out the door.

Chapter
17

I think about calling Stacey when I get home from Miss Woo's, but after avoiding her at school and then blowing up at her at dance, I'm afraid she will hang up on me.

I tromp around the house, looking for my mom so I can tell her I stood up to Stacey, just like she said I should. Only I wish she would have told me the part about how standing up to your best friend actually makes you feel about as tall as a bug when she turns and runs away. And when you hear the door slam behind her, all your bug-sized brain can think about is how she will probably just keep running and running and running until she runs into a better best friend.

I go upstairs, but before I can find my mom, I find the attic door. I go up the narrow steps and walk over to the mermaid. "Stacey said you'd make things better," I tell her. "But, the truth is, things were already pretty great before you came along. I had a new best friend. Most of the other kids were being nice to me. I got that one run in kickball. But now things are going bad and it's all your fault."

I wait for the mermaid to give me an *I'm sorry* look. But all she gives me is her same plastic smile.

I trudge down the attic steps and into my room. I fall onto my bed and hug George tight.

The next morning when I get to school, I wait around outside until the bell rings. I disappear into the crowded hallway and count floor tiles all the way to my classroom so I won't accidentally look up and see Stacey scowling at me. But when I get to my classroom, I walk right into a purple backpack that is still attached to someone.

I glance up and see dark, curly hair. Then I see Stacey's face whip a look back at me and it doesn't look one bit happy.

"Oh . . . I-Ida. It's . . . um . . . you," she says, like she's already mostly forgotten who I am.

"Um...yeah," I say back. Then I hurry past her and toss my stuff onto a coat hook and go to my desk and duck behind its lid.

When Mr. Crow makes me put my desk top down, I study the New Jersey scar on the back of Zane's head and wish that I could fly there. And no matter how hard I try to keep my eyes glued to the math problems Mr. Crow is writing on the chalkboard, they keep slipping to the side and stealing looks at Stacey's stone-still face.

I spend recess in the fourth stall of the girls' bathroom because I know I won't run into Stacey there. When I see her in the hall I walk the other way. I eat lunch with the boys.

When Mr. Crow asks us to write a paragraph using three of our spelling words, I write something else instead.

> Stacey,
> I'm sorry I've been avoiding you lately. And I'm sorry I yelled at you.
> Please don't be mad forever because that's a really long time.
>
> I.

157

I read what I wrote and then glance at Stacey. She stiffens up, so I know she sees me glancing. She doesn't glance back.

I stuff the note inside my pocket.

When it's time to go home, I grab my backpack and hurry to the bus. I find an empty seat near the back and slump in. I look out the window and see Stacey walking to the corner. She stands there, looking down the street, waiting for her dad to come and take her away for the weekend.

Two green braids plop into the seat in front of me. They are attached to the back of Jenna Drews's head. I glance at Stacey again. Then I look at Jenna.

I lean over the back of her seat. "Look," I say. "I'm sorry about the other day. I didn't plan to sneak away from your house. And I really would have liked to help paint the box even if I'm not that crazy about wearing it. And I wasn't trying to be mean when I called you Henna Jenna. Okay, maybe I was. A little. But I didn't mean for other kids to start teasing you, too."

Red spots appear on Jenna's neck. They spread up to her cheeks. And ears.

I glance out the window again. I see Stacey wave at a car that's driving down the street. It pulls up to the curb and Stacey hurries toward it.

I turn back to Jenna. "I need you to do something for me," I say.

Jenna turns toward me and squints. "What?"

I pull the note out of my pocket. "Give this to Stacey for me? Please? Before she leaves?"

I look out the window. So does Jenna. Stacey tosses her school stuff into the back of her dad's car. Then she opens the front door and climbs in.

I gulp and turn back to Jenna. "I'll pay you back," I say quickly. "Anything you want. I promise."

Jenna huffs. "You can't pay me back," she says. "Good deeds don't work that way."

She grabs the note and barges off the bus.

Chapter

18

I wake up early the next morning, even though it's Saturday. I'm still thinking about what happened after school yesterday. Stacey's car pulling away from the curb. Jenna running down the sidewalk, waving and yelling. The car's brake lights coming on and Jenna shoving the note through the open window. The car driving away and Jenna running back to the bus. Red face. Green braids flying.

I'm thinking about the sticky note Rachel pressed into my hand when we got off the bus. This time, there weren't any pretend words scribbled on it. Instead it had a drawing of a stick-dad and a stick-mom with capital O mouths and shout lines coming out of them.

It was just a little drawing, but it felt big in my hand and made me wonder if Rachel could use a break from all those sticky notes. And if maybe Jenna could, too.

And then I started thinking about what Jenna said. About not being able to pay back a good deed. And that's why it takes me half the day to ask my parents if I can call Jenna and invite her to sleep over. I have to be sure I'm not doing it to pay her back.

Dad turns off the garden hose. Mom looks up from her hedge trimmers.

"You want Jenna to sleep over?" Mom asks.

I nod. "And Rachel, too, if she wants."

Mom glances at Dad. He glances back. "Well, of course, you can invite them," Mom says. "I'm just a little surprised. I didn't think Jenna was one of your best friends."

"She's not," I say. "But you don't have to be best friends to sleep over."

My mom gives me half a smile.

So does my dad.

I head for the phone.

An hour later the doorbell rings. There stands Jenna and Rachel with their backpacks and sleeping bags. Mrs. Drews is standing with them.

"Hello, Ida," Mrs. Drews says. "Long time no see."

"Actually, I saw you a couple weeks ago at Brooke's birthday party. Only you might not have seen me. I was wearing an outhouse."

"Ah, yes," Mrs. Drews replies. "That was only two weeks ago? It seems longer." Her voice trails off.

"Hi, Paula," Mom says, walking up behind me.

"Hello, Abby," Mrs. Drews replies. "Thanks for inviting the girls. I've been so busy lately, it will be nice for Paul and me to have a little down time."

"No need to thank me, Paula," Mom says. "It was Ida's idea."

Mrs. Drews looks at me. "Well, then. Thank you, Ida."

"You're welcome," I say back.

Mom convinces Mrs. Drews to stay for a cup of coffee. I lead Jenna and Rachel upstairs to my room. "What do you want to do?" I ask.

"Let's play princess!" Rachel says. She opens up her backpack and pulls out an alligator hand puppet, glittery crown, plastic dagger, and about a mile of purple netting. She drapes the netting over my desk. "This can be our castle," she says. Then she sticks George into the alligator's mouth and shoves him halfway under my bed. "And that's the dragon's lair." She puts on the crown and picks up the dagger. "Ready?" she asks.

I glance at Jenna. She glances back. "Okay," we say at the same time.

After we help Rachel rescue George from the dragon, three poisonous pencils, and a monkey-eating shoe, we go downstairs. Mrs. Drews is gone and a pan of brownies is cooling on the cupboard. We give my mom a hand eating half of them.

"You can take some home tomorrow for a treat," Mom says to Jenna and Rachel. "Your mom mentioned how busy things have been lately, so I'll put together a spinach lasagna, too."

Even though spinach lasagna doesn't sound like much of a treat to me, it must be better than whatever Mr. Drews has been bringing home from the bait shop because Jenna and Rachel give my mom a couple of big smiles.

Later, Rachel is snoring softly in a sleeping bag by my bed when me and Jenna trudge upstairs from watching a movie. I take out my barrettes and climb into bed while Jenna sits down on her sleeping bag and unbraids her hair. It's all wavy, like it was for Brooke's party. It makes her head look different. In fact, all of her looks different. Maybe it's her Tinker Bell pajamas, or her fluffy sleeping bag, or the purple glow from my desk lamp that's draped with princess netting. Whatever it is, some of Jenna's hard edges look rubbed off.

"What are you looking at?" Jenna asks.

"Oh...um...nothing," I reply. "You just look...different."

Jenna sets down her hair bands and gives me a squint. "Different?"

"Yeah," I say. "I think it's...um...your hair. It's not so green anymore."

Jenna lifts a strand of her hair and studies it for a moment. "Really?" she says.

"Really," I say back. "I think it's fading."

Jenna studies another strand. And another. Then she gives me half a smile. "I think you're right."

I give Jenna half a smile back, partly because

that's the polite thing to do and partly because this is the first time Jenna Drews has ever said I was right about anything.

Jenna crawls inside her sleeping bag. We both stare up at the ceiling for a while.

"Ida?" Jenna says. "Can you keep a secret?"

I think about the secrets I've been keeping lately. Evil mermaid spells. Stacey skipping a weekend with her dad. Sneaking around in my attic. "Usually," I say.

Jenna rolls over onto her side and looks up at me. "My dad isn't taking time off from work. He lost his job. So my mom had to get one. Two, actually. She keeps telling me not to worry. That it's just a little bump in the road and that things will be back to normal soon. Then, at night, I hear them arguing, like things are a lot bumpier than they're telling me."

Jenna rolls onto her back and stares at the ceiling again. Her face looks stone still, but her eyes look soft and wet like clay.

Suddenly, I want to say, "Guess what? I have a secret, too. There's a shrine in my attic with an evil mermaid and everything. Want to see?"

But instead I just look back at the ceiling. "I won't tell," I finally say.

"Thanks," Jenna says back.

I must fall asleep for a while because when I open my eyes again someone has turned off my desk lamp and Jenna is snoring softly next to Rachel.

I creep out of my room and tiptoe up the attic steps. I turn on the light and walk over to the mermaid. I plug her in. Then I pick her up and look her right in the evil eye.

"I just wanted you to know that I don't think you're so powerful anymore."

Her glow warms my hand, but when I set her down it hardly tingles at all.

I pick up all the plastic spiders and doll body parts and toss them onto a shelf. I crumple up the foil and throw it away. Then I carry the jar of purple water to the bathroom and dump it out. I put away the roll of toilet paper.

I go back to the attic and unplug the mermaid. I set her on a shelf with all the other stuff. Then I take out her lightbulb. Just to be sure.

I creep down the attic steps, but I don't go back to bed.

I tiptoe into my parents' bedroom instead.

I poke the lump that is closest to me. It groans and rolls over. So I walk around the bed and poke the other lump. Harder.

My mom shoots up like her hips are springs.

"I-Ida?" she says. "W-what is it? Is something wrong?"

"No," I say. "I just wanted to remind you about something."

My mom looks at the clock on her nightstand. The one, five, nine changes to a two, zero, zero. She lets her head fall back onto her pillow. I wait while she rubs her eyes. "What?" she finally asks.

"I'm nine, you know."

Mom cracks an eye at me. "I know."

"Which means I'm getting pretty big now. So you should probably start telling me about big things."

"What big things, Ida?"

"I want to know about any bumpy roads we might be experiencing. The ones that cause a lot of fighting."

My mom nudges herself up onto an elbow. She studies me through half-closed eyes. "Ida, no one is experiencing bumpy roads and no one is fighting," she says.

"Some people are," I say.

"Who?" Mom asks.

I fidget a little, remembering my promise. "Well, obviously, *someone* is. *Somewhere.* But if there was any bumpiness in our family you would tell me, right?"

My mom is quiet for a moment. Then she says, "Yes, Ida. I would tell you."

"Okay, then," I say. "That's all for now."

I start to walk away. Then I stop and turn around. "Me and Stacey play in our attic sometimes. I thought you should know."

Mom smiles. "Thanks for telling me."

"You're welcome."

19

When Dad and I get back from driving Jenna, Rachel, a spinach lasagna, and a bunch of brownies home the next day, there's a bike in my yard. And a surprise on my porch.

Stacey.

"I'm done being grounded," she says after my dad goes inside.

"I see that," I say back.

"I'm sorry I was avoiding you on Friday. I was afraid you were still mad at me."

"You were avoiding me?" I say. "I was avoiding you. I thought you were mad after I yelled at you and everything."

Stacey smiles a little. "I wasn't mad. I was just...upset. Because I knew you were right about telling the truth to my dad. Which I did."

"You did?"

Stacey nods. "When we were driving to his place I told him that our program hadn't really been canceled and that I was sorry I had lied and that I hoped he could still come. And then I told him I was afraid to invite Tanya because it might make Kelli sad to see how happy he is with her. And then I told him I was tired of not telling Kelli the truth about everything that's going on with Tanya, and with my brother, Jake, almost never being around."

"Wow, you said all that?"

Stacey nods. "It was hard, but I did it."

"What did he say?"

"Nothing, at first," Stacey replies. "When we got to his apartment he called Kelli and they talked for a long time. When he got off the phone, he gave me a hug and told me I didn't have to keep secrets from her anymore."

Stacey is quiet for a moment. Then she says, "Ida? I'm sorry about all the lies. I know the mermaid can't make things happen."

"That's okay," I say.

After Stacey bikes home, I go upstairs to get

ready for the program. And that's when I find another surprise.

A bright orange leotard is sitting on George's lap.

So is a note.

Ida,

Some mountains have volcanoes hidden inside (I know because I researched it). The real Mount Ida doesn't, but you can still wear my orange leotard and pretend you are lava inside your costume. If you want.

Jenna

P.S. Thank you for inviting us to sleep over. We had a good time.

At the bottom of the note there's a drawing of me, shooting out of a mountain. It makes me laugh. And then I laugh again because I'm pretty sure this is the first time Jenna Drews has ever made me laugh about anything.

When Mom, Dad, and I get to the dance studio later, Mr. Crow and Miss Woo are standing in the entrance, greeting everyone as they arrive. Mr. Crow is wearing a toga and sandals. And very hairy legs. Miss Woo is wearing a toga and sandals, too, only it's a much better look on her. Trust me.

I peek inside the studio and see chairs set up all around the edge. Painted cardboard pillars stand in each corner and a table full of Greek food—grapes, olives, cheese, crackers, and punch—is set up in front of the wall of mirrors.

"Want to help hand out olive branches?" I hear someone say.

I turn around and see Tom Sanders. He's wearing a shiny gold toga and holding a bunch of fake olive-branch crowns.

"Sure," I say, taking some of the crowns. I give two to my parents. They put them on and head to the food table. I give more crowns to Jolene's family when they arrive. And Meeka's. And Randi's. Pretty soon the whole place is crawling with people who have leaves sticking out of their hair.

I'm down to three crowns when Mr. and Mrs. Drews arrive with Rachel and Jenna. Rachel is wearing her blue tutu and carrying a lumpy plastic bag. Jenna is wearing her green leotard and vines. I see her glance at the bright orange leotard

I'm wearing under my white hoodie. Even though her face is painted with bugs and butterflies, I can still see her grin.

"Thanks, Ida," Mr. Drews says as I hand him and Mrs. Drews their crowns. "And thank your mom for the spinach lasagna. It was delicious."

"You can thank her yourself," I say, looking toward the food table.

"We'll do that," Mrs. Drews says, taking Mr. Drews's arm and heading inside.

I feel a tug on my sleeve. "I want to wear a stick," Rachel says, eyeing my last olive-branch crown.

"No, Rachel," Jenna says. "You're *in* the program. Those are only for the people who watch."

"I gotta watch," Rachel says, holding up her wrist. Her frog's tongue ticks off the seconds.

Jenna rolls her eyes. "That doesn't count."

"It does, too," Rachel says, pointing to the numbers. "And so do I."

She takes the crown from me and puts it on her head.

"It's almost time to start," Mr. Crow tells us. "I want everyone to gather off stage until it's your turn to perform." He points to a room that's hooked to the studio. I see Mount Ida waiting inside.

We all head to the room. I pull up my hoodie and slip on my box.

"Where's Stacey?" Jenna asks, glancing around the room.

I glance around, too. "Don't worry," I say. "She'll be here."

"She better be," Jenna says.

Mr. Crow walks to the center of the studio and greets everyone. "We'd like to begin our program with a poem written by Stacey Merriweather. Mr. Crow looks around. "Is Stacey here?"

"Right here!" Stacey runs into the studio from outside. So do Kelli and Grandma Tootie. And a man with dark eyes and curly hair, just like Stacey's. And a woman who's holding his hand. And a bigger boy with spiky blond hair, like Kelli's.

"Here, Jake," Stacey says, tossing the boy her jacket. "Hold this."

"What am I? Your servant?" he asks.

"Servant, brother, same thing," Stacey replies.

Kelli laughs. So does Grandma Tootie. And Stacey's dad. And Tanya.

Stacey hurries over to Mr. Crow.

"Sorry I'm late," she says.

"You're right on time," Mr. Crow replies. "Ready?"

Stacey nods and unfolds a piece of paper. She smiles at her family. Then she starts reading.

In ancient times when Earth was new,
The goddess Gaia knew what to do.
She made more gods right on the spot.
Her husband, Sky, helped out a lot.

The god Poseidon made men flee
Each time his trident hit the sea.
Athena with her shiny shield
Made bad guys run and armies yield.

The best at beauty was Aphrodite.
The head god, Zeus, was strong and mighty.
Strange Argus with his hundred eyes
Kept watch for sneaky tricks and lies.

As nymph or goddess, god or muse,
We're here to share some made-up news
And offer no apology
For this friendly mythology.

Everyone applauds. Stacey walks over to where I'm standing.

"That was great," I say. "I didn't know you wrote a poem for the program."

"I wrote it this weekend at my dad's," Stacey says. "Tanya even helped me. Then Kelli called Mr. Crow this afternoon to see if I could read it."

Randi and Rusty bump past me as they head into the studio.

"Watch where you're going," Jenna barks from behind me. "You almost dented Ida's box."

Randi and Rusty turn around. Six eyes look back at us—four regular and two googly.

"Sorry, Ida," Randi says. "We didn't *see* you."

"Yeah," Rusty says, pointing to his forehead. "My *eye* isn't what it used to be."

They both crack up, head on stage, and start telling jokes.

"What did the boy cyclops say to the girl cyclops?"
"You're the apple of my eye!"

"What do you call a cyclops who wears glasses?"
"Two-eyes!"

"What do you call a cyclops pirate?"
"Man overboard!"

"When do cyclops friends fight?"
"When they don't see eye to eye!"

Randi and Rusty tell a few more jokes, peel off
their googly eyes, and take a bow.

Tom takes the stage. Actually, he shoots across
it. On rollerblades. He's wearing a box that's
painted like a golden chariot. A*TOMO* is written
on the sides. Zane, Dominic, and the Dylans are
pulling him along. They're wearing basketball jer-
seys and bridles—a team of horses. Get it?

I smile as Tom zigzags across the floor because
it's funny and because it's nice to know I'm not
the only one wearing a box.

After Brooke and Meeka spell out A-P-H-R-O-
D-I-T-E and A-T-H-E-N-A using only their body
parts, Mr. Crow gives me a sign. Jenna gives me
a nudge. "Go on, Ida," she says. "We're next."

I gulp and walk to the center of the studio. I
glance around at all the smiling faces.

"This is the myth of how Gaia, goddess of the

Earth, saved baby Zeus from being eaten by his father." I bite my lip, trying to remember what else Jenna told me to say. "Starring the Do-Good Nymphs. With a special appearance by Rachel Drews as baby Zeus."

I glance at Jenna. She gives me a nod.

Miss Woo starts the music and Randi gallops up to me. She pulls three Kens and two Barbies from a plastic bag. They're wearing toilet paper togas.

I glance at Rachel and see her smile.

Randi fake-swallows the dolls. Then she pulls Rachel's stuffed poodle and a rock out of the bag and shows them to the audience. The poodle is wearing a sticky note with GOAT printed on it. The rock is wearing one that says ROCK. She fake-swallows them, too.

Jolene rolls a basketball across the floor. Randi stuffs it under her spaceship toga. She staggers around, holding her stomach.

Jenna dances out with Rachel and the nymphs. Rachel stops and waves to Mr. and Mrs. Drews even though it's not part of the dance. Nobody seems to care. The nymphs help Jenna hide Rachel inside my box with me. It's cozy, but we fit.

A moment later, Rachel crawls back out, picks

up her lightning bolt, and gives Randi a whack in the stomach. Randi coughs up the rock and the poodle.

"Barf-O-Rama!" Rusty shouts.

Everyone laughs.

Rachel gives Randi another whack and she coughs up the dolls, togas and all.

Randi falls to the floor. Rachel takes a bow. So do Jenna, Brooke, Meeka, Jolene, and Stacey. I toss off my box and take one, too.

Everyone claps like thunder.

Mr. Crow steps forward. "We have one last presentation," he says and gives Quinn a nod.

Quinn carries in a horse hanging from a long pole. Joey and Dominic whack it with wooden swords. When it finally splits open, a hundred plastic army guys spill out.

But that's not all.

Candy spills out, too.

Tons of it.

Everyone dives in.

A minute later, Randi jumps up holding a fist-ful of Choco-chunks in each hand. "Sweet!" she shouts.

I smile because I couldn't agree more.

Epilogue

Now that Greek Day is over, I have some new things to be thankful for.

- Mr. Crow started reading a new book to our class called *Black Beauty*. It's a story about a horse. Actually, it's a story *told* by a horse. No lie. When Mr. Crow is done reading it, he's taking all of us horseback riding. He says it will be a lot of fun, but if my horse starts talking to me, I'm out of there.
- Mr. Crow also got around to remembering the math quiz we never took. Normally, that wouldn't make me thankful, but I actually did pretty good.
- Me and Stacey asked Mrs. Madson if we could alphabetize her music and she said okay. It took us three recesses.